KATHERINE
MANSFIELD

THE ESCAPE
AND OTHER STORIES

PENGUIN BOOKS

PENGUIN BOOKS

Published by the Penguin Group. Penguin Books Ltd, 27 Wrights Lane, London w8 5tz, England. Penguin Books USA Inc., 375 Hudson Street, New York, New York 10014, USA. Penguin Books Australia Ltd, Ringwood, Victoria, Australia. Penguin Books Canada Ltd, 10 Alcorn Avenue, Toronto, Ontario, Canada m4v 3b2. Penguin Books (NZ) Ltd, 182–190 Wairau Road, Auckland 10, New Zealand · Penguin Books Ltd, Registered Offices: Harmondsworth, Middlesex, England · **These stories have been taken from *The Collected Stories of Katherine Mansfield*, published by Penguin Books in 1981.** This edition published 1995 · Typeset by Datix International Limited, Bungay, Suffolk. Printed in England by Clays Ltd, St Ives plc · Except in the United States of America, this book is sold subject to the condition that it shall not, by way of trade or otherwise, be lent, re-sold, hired out, or otherwise circulated without the publisher's prior consent in any form of binding or cover other than that in which it is published and without a similar condition including this condition being imposed on the subsequent purchaser · 10 9 8 7 6 5 4 3 2 1

CONTENTS

The Escape

It was his fault, wholly and solely his fault, that they had missed the train. What if the idiotic hotel people had refused to produce the bill? Wasn't that simply because he hadn't impressed upon the waiter at lunch that they must have it by two o'clock? Any other man would have sat there and refused to move until they handed it over. But no! His exquisite belief in human nature had allowed him to get up and expect one of those idiots to bring it to their room ... And then, when the *voiture* did arrive, while they were still (Oh, heavens!) waiting for change, why hadn't he seen to the arrangement of the boxes so that they could, at least, have started the moment the money had come? Had he expected her to go outside, to stand under the awning in the heat and point with her parasol? Very amusing picture of English domestic life. Even when the driver had been told how fast he had to drive he had paid no attention whatsoever – just smiled. 'Oh,' she groaned, 'if she'd been a driver she couldn't have stopped smiling herself at the absurd, ridiculous way he was urged to hurry.' And she sat back and imitated his voice: '*Allez, vite, vite*' – and begged the driver's pardon for troubling him ...

And then the station – unforgettable – with the sight of the jaunty little train shuffling away and those hideous children waving from the windows. 'Oh, why am I made to bear these things? Why am I exposed to them? ...' The glare, the flies, while they waited, and he and the stationmaster put their heads together over the time-table, trying to find this other train, which, of course, they wouldn't catch. The people who'd gathered round, and the woman who'd held up that baby with that awful, awful head ... 'Oh, to care as I care – to feel as I feel, and never to be saved anything – never to know for one moment what it was to ... to ...'

Her voice had changed. It was shaking now – crying now. She fumbled with her bag, and produced from its little maw a scented handkerchief. She put up her veil and, as though she were saying to somebody else: 'I know, my darling,' she pressed the handkerchief to her eyes.

The little bag, with its shiny, silvery jaws open, lay on her lap. He could see her powder-puff, her rouge stick, a bundle of letters, a phial of tiny black pills like seeds, a broken cigarette, a mirror, white ivory tablets with lists on them that had been heavily scored through. He thought: 'In Egypt she would be buried with those things.'

They had left the last of the houses, those small straggling houses with bits of broken pot flung among the flower-beds and half-naked hens scratching round the doorsteps. Now they were mounting a long steep road that wound round the hill and over into the next bay. The horses stumbled, pulling hard. Every five minutes, every two minutes the driver trailed the whip across them. His stout back was solid as wood; there were boils on his reddish neck, and he wore a new, a shining new straw hat ...

There was a little wind, just enough wind to blow to satin the new leaves on the fruit trees, to stroke the fine grass, to turn to silver the smoky olives – just enough wind to start in front of the carriage a whirling, twirling snatch of dust that settled on their clothes like the finest ash. When she took out her powder-puff the powder came flying over them both.

'Oh the dust,' she breathed, 'the disgusting, revolting dust.' And she put down her veil and lay back as if overcome.

'Why don't you put up your parasol?' he suggested. It was on the front seat, and he leaned forward to hand it to her. At that she suddenly sat upright and blazed again.

'Please leave my parasol alone! I don't want my parasol! And anyone who was not utterly insensitive would know that I'm far, far too exhausted to hold up a parasol. And with a wind like this tugging at it . . . Put it down at once,' she flashed, and then snatched the parasol from him, tossed it into the crumpled hood behind, and subsided, panting.

Another bend of the road, and down the hill there came a troop of little children, shrieking and giggling, little girls with sun-bleached hair, little boys in faded soldiers' caps. In their hands they carried flowers – any kind of flowers – grabbed by the head, and these they offered, running beside the carriage. Lilac, faded lilac, greeny-white snowballs, one arum lily, a handful of hyacinths. They thrust the flowers and their impish faces into the carriage; one even threw into her lap a bunch of marigolds. Poor little mice! He had his hand in his trouser pocket before her. 'For heaven's sake don't give them anything. Oh, how typical of you! Horrid little monkeys! Now they'll follow us all the way. Don't encourage them; you *would* encourage beggars'; and she hurled the bunch out of the carriage with, 'Well, do it when I'm not there, please.'

He saw the queer shock on the children's faces. They stopped running, lagged behind, and then they began to shout something, and went on shouting until the carriage had rounded yet another bend.

'Oh, how many more are there before the top of the hill is reached? The horses haven't trotted once. Surely it isn't necessary for them to walk the whole way.'

'We shall be there in a minute now,' he said, and took out his cigarette-case. At that she turned round towards him. She clasped her hands and held them against her breast; her dark eyes looked immense, imploring, behind her veil; her nostrils quivered, she bit her lip, and her head shook with a little nervous spasm. But when she spoke, her voice was quite weak and very, very calm.

'I want to ask you something. I want to beg something of you,' she said. 'I've asked you hundreds and hundreds of times before, but you've forgotten. It's such a little thing, but if you knew what it meant to me . . .' She pressed her hands together. 'But you can't know. No human creature could know and be so cruel.' And then, slowly, deliberately, gazing at him with those huge, sombre eyes: 'I beg and implore you for the last time that when we are driving together you won't smoke. If you could imagine,' she said, 'the anguish I suffer when that smoke comes floating across my face . . .'

'Very well,' he said. 'I won't. I forgot.' And he put the case back.

'Oh no,' said she, and almost began to laugh, and put the back of her hand across her eyes. 'You couldn't have forgotten. Not that.'

The wind came, blowing stronger. They were at the top of the hill. 'Hoy-yip-yip-yip,' cried the driver. They swung down the road that fell into a small valley, skirted the sea-coast at the bottom of it, and then coiled over a gentle ridge on the other side. Now there were houses again, blue-shuttered against the heat, with bright burning gardens, with geranium carpets flung over the pinkish walls. The coast-line was dark; on the edge of the sea a white silky fringe just stirred. The carriage swung down the hill, bumped, shook. 'Yi-ip,' shouted the driver. She clutched the sides of the seat, she closed her eyes, and he knew she felt this was happening on purpose; this swinging and bump-ing, this was all done – and he was responsible for it, somehow – to spite her because she had asked if they couldn't go a little faster. But just as they reached the bottom of the valley there was one tremendous lurch. The carriage nearly overturned, and he saw her eyes blaze at him, and she positively hissed, 'I suppose you are enjoying this?'

They went on. They reached the bottom of the valley, Suddenly she stood up. '*Cocher! Cocher! Arrêtez-vous!*' She turned round and looked into the crumpled hood behind. 'I knew it,' she exclaimed. 'I knew it. I heard it fall, and so did you, at that last bump.'

'What? Where?'

'My parasol. It's gone. The parasol that belonged to my mother. The parasol that I prize more than – more than . . .' She was simply beside herself. The driver turned round, his gay, broad face smiling.

'I, too, heard something,' said he, simply and gaily. 'But I thought as Monsieur and Madame said nothing . . .'

'There. You hear that. Then you must have heard it too. So *that* accounts for the extraordinary smile on your face . . .'

'Look here,' he said, 'it can't be gone. If it fell out it will be there still. Stay where you are. I'll fetch it.'

But she saw through that. Oh, how she saw through it! 'No, thank you.' And she bent her spiteful, smiling eyes upon him, regardless of the driver. 'I'll go myself. I'll walk back and find it, and trust you not to follow. For' – knowing the driver did not understand, she spoke softly, gently – 'if I don't escape from you for a minute I shall go mad.'

She stepped out of the carriage. 'My bag.' He handed it to her.

'Madame prefers . . .'

But the driver had already swung down from his seat, and was seated on the parapet reading a small newspaper. The horses stood with hanging heads. It was still. The man in the carriage stretched himself out, folded his arms. He felt the sun beat on his knees. His head was sunk on his breast. 'Hish, hish,' sounded from the sea. The wind sighed in the valley and was quiet. He felt himself, lying there, a hollow man, a parched withered man, as it were, of ashes. And the sea sounded, 'Hish, hish.'

It was then that he saw the tree, that he was conscious of its presence just inside a garden gate. It was an immense tree with a round, thick silver stem and a great arc of copper leaves that gave back the light and yet were sombre. There was something beyond the tree – a whiteness, a softness, an opaque mass, half hidden – with delicate pillars. As he looked at the tree he felt his breathing die away and he became part of the silence. It seemed to grow, it seemed to expand in the quivering heat until the great carved leaves hid the sky, and yet it was motionless. Then from within its depths or from beyond there came the sound of a woman's voice. A woman was singing. The warm untroubled voice floated upon the air, and it was all part of the silence as he was part of it. Suddenly, as the voice rose, soft, dreaming, gentle, he knew that it would come floating to him from the hidden leaves and his peace was shattered. What was happening to him? Something stirred in his breast. Something dark, something unbearable and dreadful pushed in his bosom, and like a great weed it floated, rocked ... it was warm, stifling. He tried to struggle to tear at it, and at the same moment – all was over. Deep, deep, he sank into the silence, staring at the tree and waiting for the voice that came floating, falling, until he felt himself enfolded.

In the shaking corridor of the train. It was night. The train rushed and roared through the dark. He held on with both hands to the brass rail. The door of their carriage was open.

'Do not disturb yourself, Monsieur. He will come in and sit down when he wants to. He likes – he likes – it is his habit. ... *Oui, Madame, je suis un peu souffrante* ... *Mes nerfs.* Oh, but my husband is never so happy as when he is travelling. He likes roughing it ... My husband ... My husband ...'

7

The voices murmured, murmured. They were never still. But so great was his heavenly happiness as he stood there he wished he might live for ever.

The Daughters of the Late Colonel

I

The week after was one of the busiest weeks of their lives. Even when they went to bed it was only their bodies that lay down and rested; their minds went on, thinking things out, talking things over, wondering, deciding, trying to remember where . . .

Constantia lay like a statue, her hands by her sides, her feet just overlapping each other, the sheet up to her chin. She stared at the ceiling.

'Do you think father would mind if we gave his top-hat to the porter?'

'The porter?' snapped Josephine. 'Why ever the porter? What a very extraordinary idea!'

'Because,' said Constantia slowly, 'he must often have to go to funerals. And I noticed at – at the cemetery that he only had a bowler.' She paused. 'I thought then how very much he'd appreciate a top-hat. We ought to give him a present, too. He was always very nice to father.'

'But,' cried Josephine, flouncing on her pillow and staring across the dark at Constantia, 'father's head!' And suddenly, for one awful moment, she nearly giggled. Not, of course, that she felt in the least like giggling. It must have been habit. Years ago, when they had stayed awake at night talking, their beds had simply heaved. And now the porter's head, disappearing, popped out, like a candle, under father's

9

hat ... The giggle mounted, mounted; she clenched her hands; she fought it down; she frowned fiercely at the dark and said, 'Remember,' terribly sternly.

'We can decide to-morrow,' she said.

Constantia had noticed nothing; she sighed.

'Do you think we ought to have our dressing-gowns dyed as well?'

'Black?' almost shrieked Josephine.

'Well, what else?' said Constantia. 'I was thinking – it doesn't seem quite sincere, in a way, to wear black out of doors and when we're fully dressed, and then when we're at home –'

'But nobody sees us,' said Josephine. She gave the bedclothes such a twitch that both her feet became uncovered and she had to creep up the pillows to get them well under again.

'Kate does,' said Constantia. 'And the postman very well might.'

Josephine thought of her dark-red slippers, which matched her dressing-gown, and of Constantia's favourite indefinite green ones which went with hers. Black! Two black dressing-gowns and two pairs of black woolly slippers, creeping off to the bathroom like black cats.

'I don't think it's absolutely necessary,' said she.

Silence. Then Constantia said, 'We shall have to post the papers with the notice in them tomorrow to catch the Ceylon mail ... How many letters have we had up till now?'

'Twenty-three.'

Josephine had replied to them all, and twenty-three times

when she came to 'We miss our dear father so much' she had broken down and had to use her handkerchief, and on some of them even to soak up a very light-blue tear with an edge of blotting-paper. Strange! She couldn't have put it on – but twenty-three times. Even now, though, when she said over to herself sadly, 'We miss our dear father *so* much,' she could have cried if she'd wanted to.

'Have you got enough stamps?' came from Constantia.

'Oh, how can I tell?' said Josephine crossly. 'What's the good of asking me that now?'

'I was just wondering,' said Constantia mildly.

Silence again. There came a little rustle, a scurry, a hop.

'A mouse,' said Constantia.

'It can't be a mouse because there aren't any crumbs,' said Josephine.

'But it doesn't know there aren't,' said Constantia.

A spasm of pity squeezed her heart. Poor little thing! She wished she'd left a tiny piece of biscuit on the dressing-table. It was awful to think of it not finding anything. What would it do?

'I can't think how they manage to live at all,' she said slowly.

'Who?' demanded Josephine.

And Constantia said more loudly than she meant to, 'Mice.'

Josephine was furious. 'Oh, what nonsense, Con!' she said. 'What have mice got to do with it? You're asleep.'

'I don't think I am,' said Constantia. She shut her eyes to make sure. She was.

Josephine arched her spine, pulled up her knees, folded her arms so that her fists came under her ears, and pressed her cheek hard against the pillow.

II

Another thing which complicated matters was they had Nurse Andrews staying on with them that week. It was their own fault; they had asked her. It was Josephine's idea. On the morning – well, on the last morning, when the doctor had gone, Josephine had said to Constantia, 'Don't you think it would be rather nice if we asked Nurse Andrews to stay on for a week as our guest?'

'Very nice,' said Constantia.

'I thought,' went on Josephine quickly, 'I should just say this afternoon, after I've paid her, "My sister and I would be very pleased, after all you've done for us, Nurse Andrews, if you would stay on for a week as our guest." I'd have to put that in about being our guest in case –'

'Oh, but she could hardly expect to be paid!' cried Constantia.

'One never knows,' said Josephine sagely.

Nurse Andrews had, of course, jumped at the idea. But it was a bother. It meant they had to have regular sit-down meals at the proper times, whereas if they'd been alone they could just have asked Kate if she wouldn't have minded bringing them a tray wherever they were. And meal-times now that the strain was over were rather a trial.

Nurse Andrews was simply fearful about butter. Really they couldn't help feeling that about butter, at least, she took advantage of their kindness. And she had that maddening habit of asking for just an inch more bread to finish what she had on her plate, and then, at the last mouthful, absent-mindedly – of course it wasn't absent-mindedly – taking another helping. Josephine got very red when this happened, and she fastened her small, bead-like eyes on the tablecloth as if she saw a minute strange insect creeping through the web of it. But Constantia's long, pale face lengthened and set, and she gazed away – away – far over the desert, to where that line of camels unwound like a thread of wool . . .

'When I was with Lady Tukes,' said Nurse Andrews, 'she had such a dainty little contrayvance for the buttah. It was a silvah Cupid balanced on the – on the bordah of a glass dish, holding a tayny fork. And when you wanted some buttah you simply pressed his foot and he bent down and speared you a piece. It was quite a gayme.'

Josephine could hardly bear that. But 'I think those things are very extravagant' was all she said.

'But whey?' asked Nurse Andrews, beaming through her eyeglasses. 'No one, surely, would take more buttah than one wanted – would one?'

'Ring, Con,' cried Josephine. She couldn't trust herself to reply.

And proud young Kate, the enchanted princess, came in to see what the old tabbies wanted now. She snatched away their plates of mock something or other and slapped down a white, terrified blancmange.

'Jam, please, Kate,' said Josephine kindly.

Kate knelt and burst open the sideboard, lifted the lid of the jam-pot, saw it was empty, put it on the table, and stalked off.

'I'm afraid,' said Nurse Andrews a moment later, 'there isn't any.'

'Oh, what a bother!' said Josephine. She bit her lip. 'What had we better do?'

Constantia looked dubious. 'We can't disturb Kate again,' she said softly.

Nurse Andrews waited, smiling at them both. Her eyes wandered, spying at everything behind her eyeglasses. Constantia in despair went back to her camels. Josephine frowned heavily – concentrated. If it hadn't been for this idiotic woman she and Con would, of course, have eaten their blancmange without. Suddenly the idea came.

'I know,' she said. 'Marmalade. There's some marmalade in the sideboard. Get it, Con.'

'I hope,' laughed Nurse Andrews – and her laugh was like a spoon tinkling against a medicine-glass – 'I hope it's not very bittah marmalayde.'

III

But, after all, it was not long now, and then she'd be gone for good. And there was no getting over the fact that she had been very kind to father. She had nursed him day and night at the end. Indeed, both Constantia and Josephine felt privately she had rather overdone the not leaving him at the very last. For when they had gone in to say good-bye Nurse Andrews had sat beside his bed the whole time, holding his wrist and pretending to look at her watch. It couldn't have been necessary. It was so tactless, too. Supposing father had wanted to say something – something private to them. Not that he had. Oh, far from it! He lay there, purple, a dark, angry purple in the face, and never even looked at them when they came in. Then, as they were standing there, wondering what to do, he had suddenly opened one eye. Oh, what a difference it would have made, what a difference to their memory of him, how much easier to tell people about it, if he had only opened both! But no – one eye only. It glared at them a moment and then . . . went out.

IV

It had made it very awkward for them when Mr Farolles, of St John's, called the same afternoon.

'The end was quite peaceful, I trust?' were the first words he said as he glided towards them through the dark drawing-room.

'Quite,' said Josephine faintly. They both hung their heads. Both of them felt certain that eye wasn't at all a peaceful eye.

'Won't you sit down?' said Josephine.

'Thank you, Miss Pinner,' said Mr Farolles gratefully. He folded his coat-tails and began to lower himself into father's arm-chair, but just as he touched it he almost sprang up and slid into the next chair instead.

He coughed. Josephine clasped her hands; Constantia looked vague.

'I want you to feel, Miss Pinner,' said Mr Farolles, 'and you, Miss Constantia, that I'm trying to be helpful. I want to be helpful to you both, if you will let me. These are the times,' said Mr Farolles, very simply and earnestly, 'when God means us to be helpful to one another.'

'Thank you very much, Mr Farolles,' said Josephine and Constantia.

'Not at all,' said Mr Farolles gently. He drew his kid gloves through his fingers and leaned forward. 'And if either of you would like a little Communion, either or both of you, here *and* now, you have only to tell me. A little Communion is often very help – a great comfort,' he added tenderly.

But the idea of a little Communion terrified them. What! In the drawing-room by themselves – with no – no altar or anything! The piano would be much too high, thought Constantia, and Mr Farolles could not possibly lean over it with the chalice. And Kate would be sure to come bursting in and interrupt them, thought Josephine. And supposing the bell rang in the middle? It might be somebody important – about their mourning. Would they get up reverently and go out, or would they have to wait . . . in torture?

'Perhaps you will send round a note by your good Kate if you would care for it later,' said Mr Farolles.

'Oh yes, thank you very much!' they both said.

Mr Farolles got up and took his black straw hat from the round table.

'And about the funeral,' he said softly. 'I may arrange that – as your dear father's old friend and yours, Miss Pinner – and Miss Constantia?'

Josephine and Constantia got up too.

'I should like it to be quite simple,' said Josephine firmly, 'and not too expensive. At the same time, I should like –'

'A good one that will last,' thought dreamy Constantia, as if Josephine were buying a night-gown. But, of course, Josephine didn't say that. 'One suitable to our father's position.' She was very nervous.

'I'll run round to our good friend Mr Knight,' said Mr Farolles soothingly. 'I will ask him to come and see you. I am sure you will find him very helpful indeed.'

V

Well, at any rate, all that part of it was over, though neither of them could possibly believe that father was never coming back. Josephine had had a moment of absolute terror at the cemetery, while the coffin was lowered, to think that she and Constantia had done this thing without asking his permission. What would father say when he found out? For he was bound to find out sooner or later. He always did. 'Buried. You two girls had me *buried*!' She heard his stick thumping. Oh, what would they say? What possible excuse could they make? It sounded such an appallingly heartless thing to do. Such a wicked advantage to take of a person because he happened to be helpless at the moment. The other people seemed to treat it all as a matter of course. They were strangers; they couldn't be expected to understand that father was the very last person for such a thing to happen to. No, the entire blame for it all would fall on her and Constantia. And the expense, she thought, stepping into the tight-buttoned cab. When she had to show him the bills. What would he say then?

She heard him absolutely roaring. 'And do you expect me to pay for this gimcrack excursion of yours?'

'Oh,' groaned poor Josephine aloud, 'we shouldn't have done it, Con!'

And Constantia, pale as a lemon in all that blackness, said in a frightened whisper, 'Done what, Jug?'

'Let them bu-bury father like that,' said Josephine, breaking down and crying into her new, queer-smelling mourning handkerchief.

'But what else could we have done?' asked Constantia wonderingly. 'We couldn't have kept him, Jug – we couldn't have kept him unburied. At any rate, not in a flat that size.'

Josephine blew her nose; the cab was dreadfully stuffy.

'I don't know,' she said forlornly. 'It is all so dreadful. I feel we ought to have tried to, just for a time at least. To make perfectly sure. One thing's certain' – and her tears sprang out again – 'father will never forgive us for this – never!'

VI

Father would never forgive them. That was what they felt
more than ever when, two mornings later, they went into his
room to go through his things. They had discussed it quite
calmly. It was even down on Josephine's list of things to be
done. *Go through father's things and settle about them.* But that
was a very different matter from saying after breakfast:

'Well, are you ready, Con?'

'Yes, Jug – when you are.'

'Then I think we'd better get it over.'

It was dark in the hall. It been a rule for years never to
disturb father in the morning, whatever happened. And now
they were going to open the door without knocking even . . .
Constantia's eyes were enormous at the idea; Josephine felt
weak in the knees.

'You – you go first,' she gasped, pushing Constantia.

But Constantia said, as she always had said on those
occasions, 'No, Jug, that's not fair. You're eldest.'

Josephine was just going to say – what at other times she
wouldn't have owned to for the world – what she kept for her
very last weapon, 'But you're tallest,' when they noticed that
the kitchen door was open, and there stood Kate . . .

'Very stiff,' said Josephine, grasping the door-handle and
doing her best to turn it. As if anything ever deceived Kate!

It couldn't be helped. That girl was . . . Then the door
was shut behind them, but – but they weren't in father's
room at all. They might have suddenly walked through the   19

wall by mistake into a different flat altogether. Was the door just behind them? They were too frightened to look. Josephine knew that if it was it was holding itself tight shut; Constantia felt that, like the doors in dreams, it hadn't any handle at all. It was the coldness which made it so awful. Or the whiteness – which? Everything was covered. The blinds were down, a cloth hung over the mirror, a sheet hid the bed; a huge fan of white paper filled the fire-place. Constantia timidly put out her hand; she almost expected a snowflake to fall. Josephine felt a queer tingling in her nose, as if her nose was freezing. Then a cab klop-klopped over the cobbles below, and the quiet seemed to shake into little pieces.

'I had better pull up a blind,' said Josephine bravely.

'Yes, it might be a good idea,' whispered Constantia.

They only gave the blind a touch, but it flew up and the cord flew after, rolling the blind-stick, the little tassel tapped as if trying to get free. That was too much for Constantia.

'Don't you think – don't you think we might put it off for another day?' she whispered.

'Why?' snapped Josephine, feeling, as usual, much better now that she knew for certain that Constantia was terrified. 'It's got to be done. But I do wish you wouldn't whisper, Con.'

'I didn't know I was whispering,' whispered Constantia.

'And why do you keep on staring at the bed?' said Josephine, raising her voice almost defiantly. 'There's nothing *on* the bed.'

'Oh, Jug, don't say so!' said poor Connie. 'At any rate, not so loudly.'

Josephine felt herself that she had gone too far. She took a wide swerve over to the chest of drawers, put out her hand, but quickly drew it back again.

'Connie!' she gasped, and she wheeled round and leaned with her back against the chest of drawers.

'Oh, Jug – what?'

Josephine could only glare. She had the most extraordinary feeling that she had just escaped something simply awful. But how could she explain to Constantia that father was in the chest of drawers? He was in the top drawer with his handkerchiefs and neckties, or in the next with his shirts and pyjamas, or in the lowest of all with his suits. He was watching there, hidden away – just behind the door-handle – ready to spring.

She pulled a funny old-fashioned face at Constantia, just as she used to in the old days when she was going to cry.

'I can't open,' she nearly wailed.

'No, don't, Jug,' whispered Constantia earnestly. 'It's much better not to. Don't let's open anything. At any rate, not for a long time.'

'But – but it seems so weak,' said Josephine, breaking down.

'But why not be weak for once, Jug?' argued Constantia, whispering quite fiercely. 'If it is weak.' And her pale stare flew from the locked writing-table – so safe – to the huge glittering wardrobe, and she began to breathe in a queer, panting way. 'Why shouldn't we be weak for once in our lives, Jug? It's quite excusable. Let's be weak – be weak, Jug. It's much nicer to be weak than to be strong.'

And then she did one of those amazingly bold things that 21

she'd done about twice before in their lives: she marched over to the wardrobe, turned the key, and took it out of the lock. Took it out of the lock and held it up to Josephine, showing Josephine by her extraordinary smile that she knew what she'd done – she'd risked deliberately father being in there among his overcoats.

If the huge wardrobe had lurched forward, had crashed down on Constantia, Josephine wouldn't have been surprised. On the contrary, she would have thought it the only suitable thing to happen. But nothing happened. Only the room seemed quieter than ever, and bigger flakes of cold air fell on Josephine's shoulders and knees. She began to shiver.

'Come, Jug,' said Constantia, still with that awful callous smile; and Josephine followed just as she had that last time, when Constantia had pushed Benny into the round pond.

VII

But the strain told on them when they were back in the dining-room. They sat down, very shaky, and looked at each other.

'I don't feel I can settle to anything,' said Josephine, 'until I've had something. Do you think we could ask Kate for two cups of hot water?'

'I really don't see why we shouldn't,' said Constantia carefully. She was quite normal again. 'I won't ring. I'll go to the kitchen door and ask her.'

'Yes, do,' said Josephine, sinking down into a chair. 'Tell her, just two cups, Con, nothing else – on a tray.'

'She needn't even put the jug on, need she?' said Constantia, as though Kate might very well complain if the jug had been there.

'Oh no, certainly not! The jug's not at all necessary. She can pour it direct out of the kettle,' cried Josephine, feeling that would be a labour-saving indeed.

Their cold lips quivered at the greenish brims. Josephine curved her small red hands round the cup; Constantia sat up and blew on the wavy steam, making it flutter from one side to the other.

'Speaking of Benny,' said Josephine.

And though Benny hadn't been mentioned Constantia immediately looked as though he had.

'He'll expect us to send him something of father's, of course. But it's so difficult to know what to send to Ceylon.'

'You mean things get unstuck so on the voyage,' murmured Constantia.

'No, lost,' said Josephine sharply. 'You know there's no post. Only runners.'

Both paused to watch a black man in white linen drawers running through the pale fields for dear life, with a large brown-paper parcel in his hands. Josephine's black man was tiny; he scurried along glistening like an ant. But there was something blind and tireless about Constantia's tall, thin fellow, which made him, she decided, a very unpleasant person indeed . . . On the veranda, dressed all in white and wearing a cork helmet, stood Benny. His right hand shook up and down, as father's did when he was impatient. And behind him, not in the least interested, sat Hilda, the unknown sister-in-law. She swung in a cane rocker and flicked over the leaves of the *Tatler*.

'I think his watch would be the most suitable present,' said Josephine.

Constantia looked up; she seemed surprised.

'Oh, would you trust a gold watch to a native?'

'But, of course, I'd disguise it,' said Josephine. 'No one would know it was a watch.' She liked the idea of having to make a parcel such a curious shape that no one could possibly guess what it was. She even thought for a moment of hiding the watch in a narrow cardboard corset-box that she'd kept by her for a long time, waiting for it to come in for something. It was such beautiful, firm cardboard. But, no, it wouldn't be appropriate for this occasion. It had lettering on it: *Medium Women's* 28. *Extra Firm Busks*. It would be almost too much of a surprise for Benny to open that and find father's watch inside.

'And, of course, it isn't as though it would be going – ticking, I mean,' said Constantia, who was still thinking of the native love of jewellery. 'At least,' she added, 'it would be very strange if after all that time it was.'

VIII

Josephine made no reply. She had flown off on one of her tangents. She had suddenly thought of Cyril. Wasn't it more usual for the only grandson to have the watch? And then dear Cyril was so appreciative and a gold watch meant so much to a young man. Benny, in all probability, had quite got out of the habit of watches; men so seldom wore waistcoats in those hot climates. Whereas Cyril in London wore them from year's end to year's end. And it would be so nice for her and Constantia, when he came to tea, to know it was there. 'I see you've got on grandfather's watch, Cyril.' It would be somehow so satisfactory.

Dear boy! What a blow his sweet, sympathetic little note had been! Of course they quite understood; but it was most unfortunate.

'It would have been such a point, having him,' Josephine.

'And he would have enjoyed it so,' said Constantia, not thinking what she was saying.

However, as soon as he got back he was coming to tea with his aunties. Cyril to tea was one of their rare treats.

'Now, Cyril, you mustn't be frightened of our cakes. Your Auntie Con and I bought them at Buszard's this morning. We know what a man's appetite is. So don't be ashamed of making a good tea.'

Josephine cut recklessly into the rich dark cake that stood for her winter gloves or the soling and heeling of Constantia's only respectable shoes. But Cyril was most unmanlike in appetite.

'I say, Aunt Josephine, I simply can't. I've only just had lunch, you know.'

'Oh, Cyril, that can't be true! It's after four,' cried Josephine. Constantia sat with her knife poised over the chocolate-roll. 25

'It is, all the same,' said Cyril. 'I had to meet a man at Victoria, and he kept me hanging about till . . . there was only time to get lunch and to come on here. And he gave me – phew' – Cyril put his hand to his forehead – 'a terrific blow-out,' he said.

It was disappointing – today of all days. But still he couldn't be expected to know.

'But you'll have a meringue, won't you, Cyril?' said Aunt Josephine. 'These meringues were bought specially for you. Your dear father was so fond of them. We were sure you are, too.'

'I *am*, Aunt Josephine,' cried Cyril ardently. 'Do you mind if I take half to begin with?'

'Not at all, dear boy; but we mustn't let you off with that.'

'Is your dear father still so fond of meringues?' asked Auntie Con gently. She winced faintly as she broke through the shell of hers.

'Well, I don't quite know, Auntie Con,' said Cyril breezily.

At that they both looked up.

'Don't know?' almost snapped Josephine. 'Don't know a thing like that about your own father, Cyril?'

'Surely,' said Auntie Con softly.

Cyril tried to laugh it off. 'Oh, well,' he said, 'it's such a long time since –' He faltered. He stopped. Their faces were too much for him.

'Even *so*,' said Josephine.

And Auntie Con looked.

Cyril put down his teacup. 'Wait a bit,' he cried. 'Wait a bit, Aunt Josephine. What am I thinking of?'

He looked up. They were beginning to brighten. Cyril slapped his knee.

'Of course,' he said, 'it was meringues. How could I have forgotten? Yes, Aunt Josephine, you're perfectly right. Father's most frightfully keen on meringues.'

They didn't only beam. Aunt Josephine went scarlet with pleasure; Auntie Con gave a deep, deep sigh.

'And now, Cyril, you must come and see father,' said Josephine. 'He knows you were coming today.'

'Right,' said Cyril, very firmly and heartily. He got up from his chair; suddenly he glanced at the clock.

'I say, Auntie Con, isn't your clock a bit slow? I've got to meet a man at – at Paddington just after five. I'm afraid I shan't be able to stay very long with grandfather.'

'Oh, he won't expect you to stay *very* long!' said Aunt Josephine.

Constantia was still gazing at the clock. She couldn't make up her mind if it was fast or slow. It was one or the other, she felt almost certain of that. At any rate, it had been.

Cyril still lingered. 'Aren't you coming along, Auntie Con?'

'Of course,' said Josephine, 'we shall all go. Come on, Con.'

IX

They knocked at the door, and Cyril followed his aunts into grandfather's hot, sweetish room.

27

'Come on,' said Grandfather Pinner. 'Don't hang about. What is it? What've you been up to?'

He was sitting in front of a roaring fire, clasping his stick. He had a thick rug over his knees. On his lap there lay a beautiful pale-yellow silk handkerchief.

'It's Cyril, father,' said Josephine shyly. And she took Cyril's hand and led him forward.

'Good afternoon, grandfather,' said Cyril, trying to take his hand out of Aunt Josephine's. Grandfather Pinner shot his eyes at Cyril in the way he was famous for. Where was Auntie Con? She stood on the other side of Aunt Josephine; her long arms hung down in front of her; her hands were clasped. She never took her eyes off grandfather.

'Well,' said Grandfather Pinner, beginning to thump, 'what have you got to tell me?'

What had he, what had he got to tell him? Cyril felt himself smiling like a perfect imbecile. The room was stifling, too.

But Aunt Josephine came to his rescue. She cried brightly, 'Cyril says his father is still very fond of meringues, father dear.'

'Eh?' said Grandfather Pinner, curving his hand like a purple meringue-shell over one ear.

Josephine repeated, 'Cyril says his father is still very fond of meringues.'

'Can't hear,' said old Colonel Pinner. And he waved Josephine away with his stick, then pointed with his stick to Cyril. 'Tell me what she's trying to say,' he said.

(My God!) 'Must I?' said Cyril, blushing and staring at
Aunt Josephine.

'Do, dear,' she smiled. 'It will please him so much.'

'Come on, out with it!' cried Colonel Pinner testily, beginning to thump again.

And Cyril leaned forward and yelled, 'Father's still very fond of meringues.'

At that Grandfather Pinner jumped as though he had been shot.

'Don't shout!' he cried. 'What's the matter with the boy? *Meringues!* What about 'em?'

'Oh, Aunt Josephine, must we go on?' groaned Cyril desperately.

'It's quite all right, dear boy,' said Aunt Josephine, as though he and she were at the dentist's together. 'He'll understand in a minute.' And she whispered to Cyril, 'He's getting a bit deaf, you know.' Then she leaned forward and really bawled at Grandfather Pinner, 'Cyril only wanted to tell you, father dear, that *his* father is still very fond of meringues.'

Colonel Pinner heard that time, heard and brooded, looking Cyril up and down.

'What an esstrordinary thing!' said old Grandfather Pinner. 'What an esstrordinary thing to come all this way here to tell me!'

And Cyril felt it *was.*

'Yes, I shall send Cyril the watch,' said Josephine.

'That would be very nice,' said Constantia. 'I seem to remember last time he came there was some little trouble about the time.'

They were interrupted by Kate bursting through the door in her usual fashion, as though she had discovered some secret panel in the wall.

'Fried or boiled?' asked the bold voice.

Fried or boiled? Josephine and Constantia were quite bewildered for the moment. They could hardly take it in.

'Fried or boiled what, Kate?' asked Josephine, trying to begin to concentrate.

Kate gave a loud sniff. 'Fish.'

'Well, why didn't you say something immediately?' Josephine reproached her gently. 'How could you expect us to understand, Kate? There are a great many things in this world, you know, which are fried or boiled.' And after such a display of courage she said quite brightly to Constantia, 'Which do you prefer, Con?'

'I think it might be nice to have it fried,' said Constantia. 'On the other hand, of course, boiled fish is very nice. I think I prefer both equally well ... Unless you ... In that case –'

'I shall fry it,' said Kate, and she bounced back, leaving their door open and slamming the door of her kitchen.

Josephine gazed at Constantia; she raised her pale eyebrows until they rippled away into her pale hair. She got up. She said in a very lofty, imposing way, 'Do you mind following me into the drawing-room, Constantia? I've something of great importance to discuss with you.'

For it was always to the drawing-room they retired when they wanted to talk over Kate.

Josephine closed the door meaningly. 'Sit down, Constantia,' she said, very grand. She might have been receiving Constantia for the first time. And Con looked vaguely for a chair, as though she felt indeed quite a stranger.

'Now the question is,' said Josephine, bending forward, 'whether we shall keep her or not.'

'That is the question,' agreed Constantia.

'And this time,' said Josephine firmly, 'we must come to a definite decision.'

Constantia looked for a moment as though she might begin going over all the other times, but she pulled herself together and said, 'Yes, Jug.'

'You see, Con,' explained Josephine, 'everything is so changed now.' Constantia looked up quickly. 'I mean,' went on Josephine, 'we're not dependent on Kate as we were.' And she blushed faintly. 'There's not father to cook for.'

'That is perfectly true,' agreed Constantia. 'Father certainly doesn't want any cooking now whatever else –'

Josephine broke in sharply, 'You're not sleepy, are you, Con.'

'Sleepy, Jug?' Constantia was wide-eyed.

'Well, concentrate more,' said Josephine sharply, and she returned to the subject. 'What it comes to is, if we did' – and this she barely breathed, glancing at the door – 'give Kate notice' – she raised her voice again – 'we could manage our own food.'

'Why not?' cried Constantia. She couldn't help smiling. 31

The idea was so exciting. She clasped her hands. 'What should we live on, Jug?'

'Oh, eggs in various forms!' said Jug, lofty again. 'And, besides, there are all the cooked foods.'

'But I've always heard,' said Constantia, 'they are considered so very expensive.'

'Not if one buys them in moderation,' said Josephine. But she tore herself away from this fascinating bypath and dragged Constantia after her.

'What we've got to decide now, however, is whether we really do trust Kate or not.'

Constantia leaned back. Her flat little laugh flew from her lips.

'Isn't it curious, Jug,' said she, 'that just on this one subject I've never been able to quite make up my mind?'

XI

She never had. The whole difficulty was to prove anything. How did one prove things, how could one? Suppose Kate had stood in front of her and deliberately made a face. Mightn't she very well have been in pain? Wasn't it impossible, at any rate, to ask Kate if she was making a face at her? If Kate answered 'No' – and, of course, she would say 'No' – what a position! How undignified! Then, again, Constantia suspected, she was almost certain that Kate went to her chest of drawers when she and Josephine were out, not to take things but to spy. Many times she had come back to find her
amethyst cross in the most unlikely places, under her lace ties

or on top of her evening Bertha. More than once she had laid a trap for Kate. She had arranged things in a special order and then called Josephine to witness.

'You see, Jug?'

'Quite, Con.'

'Now we shall be able to tell.'

But, oh dear, when she did go to look, she was as far off from a proof as ever! If anything was displaced, it might so very well have happened as she closed the drawer; a jolt might have done it so easily.

'You come, Jug, and decide. I really can't. It's too difficult.'

But after a pause and a long glare Josephine would sigh, 'Now you've put the doubt into my mind, Con, I'm sure I can't tell myself.'

'Well, we can't postpone it again,' said Josephine. 'If we postpone it this time –'

XII

But at that moment in the street below a barrel-organ struck up. Josephine and Constantia sprang to their feet together.

'Run, Con,' said Josephine. 'Run quickly. There's sixpence on the –'

Then they remembered. It didn't matter. They would never have to stop the organ-grinder again. Never again would she and Constantia be told to make that monkey take his noise somewhere else. Never would sound that loud,   33 strange bellow when father thought they were not hurrying enough. The organ-grinder might play there all day and the stick would not thump.

> It never will thump again,
> It never will thump again,

played the barrel-organ.

What was Constantia thinking? She had such a strange smile; she looked different. She couldn't be going to cry.

'Jug, Jug,' said Constantia softly, pressing her hands together. 'Do you know what day it is? It's Saturday. It's a week today, a whole week.'

> A week since father died,
> A week since father died,

cried the barrel-organ. And Josephine, too, forgot to be practical and sensible; she smiled faintly, strangely. On the Indian carpet there fell a square of sunlight, pale red; it came and went and came – and stayed, deepened – until it shone almost golden.

'The sun's out,' said Josephine, as though it really mattered.

A perfect fountain of bubbling notes shook from the barrel-organ, round, bright notes, carelessly scattered.

Constantia lifted her big, cold hands as if to catch them, and then her hands fell again. She walked over to the mantelpiece to her favourite Buddha. And the stone and gilt image, whose smile always gave her such a queer feeling, almost a pain and yet a pleasant pain, seemed today to be more than smiling. He knew something; he had a secret. 'I know something that you don't know,' said her Buddha. Oh, what was it, what could it be? And yet she had always felt there was . . . something.

The sunlight pressed through the windows, thieved its way in, flashed its light over the furniture and the photographs. Josephine watched it. When it came to mother's photograph, the enlargement over the piano, it lingered as though puzzled to find so little remained of mother, except the ear-rings shaped like tiny pagodas and a black feather boa. Why did the photographs of dead people always fade so? wondered Josephine. As soon as a person was dead their photograph died too. But, of course, this one of mother was very old. It was thirty-five years old. Josephine remembered standing on a chair and pointing out that feather boa to Constantia and telling her that it was a snake that had killed their mother in Ceylon . . . Would everything have been different if mother hadn't died? She didn't see why. Aunt Florence had lived with them until they had left school, and they had moved three times and had their yearly holiday and . . and there'd been changes of servants, of course.

Some little sparrows, young sparrows they sounded, chirped on the window-ledge. *Yeep – eyeep – yeep.* But Josephine felt they were not sparrows, not on the window-ledge. It was inside her, that queer little crying noise. *Yeep – eyeep – yeep.* Ah, what was it crying, so weak and forlorn?

If mother had lived, might they have married? But there had been nobody for them to marry. There had been father's Anglo-Indian friends before he quarrelled with them. But

35

after that she and Constantia never met a single man except clergymen. How did one meet men? Or even if they'd met them, how could they have got to know men well enough to be more than strangers? One read of people having adventures, being followed, and so on. But nobody had ever followed Constantia and her. Oh yes, there had been one year at Eastbourne a mysterious man at their boarding-house who had put a note on the jug of hot water outside their bedroom door! But by the time Connie had found it the steam had made the writing too faint to read; they couldn't even make out to which of them it was addressed. And he had left next day. And that was all. The rest had been looking after father and at the same time keeping out of father's way. But now? But now? The thieving sun touched Josephine gently. She lifted her face. She was drawn over to the window by gentle beams . . .

Until the barrel-organ stopped playing Constantia stayed before the Buddha, wondering, but not as usual, not vaguely. This time her wonder was like longing. She remembered the times she had come in here, crept out of bed in her night-gown when the moon was full, and lain on the floor with her arms outstretched, as though she was crucified. Why? The big, pale moon had made her do it. The horrible dancing figures on the carved screen had leered at her and she hadn't minded. She remembered too how, whenever they were at the seaside, she had gone off by herself and got as close to the sea as she could, and sung something, something she had made up, while she gazed all over that restless water. There had been this other life, running out, bringing things home in bags, getting things on approval, discussing them with Jug, and taking them back to get more things on approval, and arranging father's trays and trying not to annoy father. But it all seemed to have happened in a kind of tunnel. It wasn't real. It was only when she came out of the tunnel into the moonlight or by the sea or into a thunderstorm that she really felt herself. What did it mean? What was it she was always wanting? What did it all lead to? Now? Now?

She turned away from the Buddha with one of her vague gestures. She went over to where Josephine was standing. She wanted to say something to Josephine, something frightfully important, about – about the future and what . . .

'Don't you think perhaps –' she began.

But Josephine interrupted her. 'I was wondering if now –' she murmured. They stopped; they waited for each other.

'Go on, Con,' said Josephine.

'No, no, Jug; after you,' said Constantia.

'No, say what you were going to say. You began,' said Josephine.

'I . . . I'd rather hear what you were going to say first,' said Constantia.

'Don't be absurd, Con.'

'Really, Jug.'

'Connie!'

'Oh, *Jug*!'

A pause. Then Constantia said faintly, 'I can't say what I was going to say, Jug, because I've forgotten what it was . . . that I was going to say.'

Josephine was silent for a moment. She stared at a big cloud where the sun had been. Then she replied shortly, 'I've forgotten too.'

The Garden-party

And after all the weather was ideal. They could not have had a more perfect day for a garden-party if they had ordered it. Windless, warm, the sky without a cloud. Only the blue was veiled with a haze of light gold, as it is sometimes in early summer. The gardener had been up since dawn, mowing the lawns and sweeping them, until the grass and the dark flat rosettes where the daisy plants had been seemed to shine. As for the roses, you could not help feeling they understood that roses are the only flowers that impress people at garden-parties; the only flowers that everybody is certain of knowing. Hundreds, yes, literally hundreds, had come out in a single night; the green bushes bowed down as though they had been visited by archangels.

Breakfast was not yet over before the men came to put up the marquee.

'Where do you want the marquee put, mother?'

'My dear child, it's no use asking me. I'm determined to leave everything to you children this year. Forget I am your mother. Treat me as an honoured guest.'

But Meg could not possibly go and supervise the men. She had washed her hair before breakfast, and she sat drinking her coffee in a green turban, with a dark wet curl stamped on each cheek. Jose, the butterfly, always came down in a silk petticoat and a kimono jacket.

'You'll have to go, Laura; you're the artistic one.'

Away Laura flew, still holding her piece of bread-and-butter. It's so delicious to have an excuse for eating out of doors and, besides, she loved having to arrange things; she always felt she could do it so much better than anybody else.

Four men in their shirt-sleeves stood grouped together on the garden path. They carried staves covered with rolls of canvas and they had big tool-bags slung on their backs. They looked impressive. Laura wished now that she was not holding that piece of bread-and-butter, but there was nowhere to put it and she couldn't possibly throw it away. She blushed and tried to look severe and even a little bit short-sighted as she came up to them.

'Good morning,' she said, copying her mother's voice. But that sounded so fearfully affected that she was ashamed, and stammered like a little girl, 'Oh – er – have you come – is it about the marquee?'

'That's right, miss,' said the tallest of the men, a lanky, freckled fellow, and he shifted his tool-bag, knocked back his straw hat and smiled down at her. 'That's about it.'

His smile was so easy, so friendly, that Laura recovered. What nice eyes he had, small, but such a dark blue! And now she looked at the others, they were smiling too! 'Cheer up, we won't bite,' their smile seemed to say. How very nice workmen were! And what a beautiful morning! She mustn't mention the morning; she must be business-like. The marquee.

'Well, what about the lily-lawn? Would that do?'

And she pointed to the lily-lawn with the hand that didn't

hold the bread-and-butter. They turned, they stared in the direction. A little fat chap thrust out his underlip and the tall fellow frowned.

'I don't fancy it,' said he. 'Not conspicuous enough. You see, with a thing like a marquee' – and he turned to Laura in his easy way – 'you want to put it somewhere where it'll give you a bang slap in the eye, if you follow me.'

Laura's upbringing made her wonder for a moment whether it was quite respectful of a workman to talk to her of bangs slap in the eye. But she did quite follow him.

'A corner of the tennis-court,' she suggested. 'But the band's going to be in one corner.'

'H'm, going to have a band, are you?' said another of the workmen. He was pale. He had a haggard look as his dark eyes scanned the tennis-court. What was he thinking?

'Only a very small band,' said Laura gently. Perhaps he wouldn't mind so much if the band was quite small. But the tall fellow interrupted.

'Look here, miss, that's the place. Against those trees. Over there. That'll do fine.'

Against the karakas. Then the karaka trees would be hidden. And they were so lovely, with their broad, gleaming leaves, and their clusters of yellow fruit. They were like trees you imagined growing on a desert island, proud, solitary, lifting their leaves and fruits to the sun in a kind of silent splendour. Must they be hidden by a marquee?

They must. Already the men had shouldered their staves and were making for the place. Only the tall fellow was left. He bent down, pinched a sprig of lavender, put his thumb and forefinger to his nose and snuffed up the smell. When Laura saw that gesture she forgot all about the karakas in her wonder at him caring for things like that – caring for the smell of lavender. How many men that she knew would have done such a thing. Oh, how extraordinarily nice workmen were, she thought. Why couldn't she have workmen for friends rather than the silly boys she danced with and who came to Sunday night supper? She would get on much better with men like these.

It's all the fault, she decided, as the tall fellow drew something on the back of an envelope, something that was to be looped up or left to hang, of these absurd class distinctions. Well, for her part, she didn't feel them. Not a bit, not an atom . . . And now there came the chock-chock of wooden hammers. Someone whistled, someone sang out, 'Are you right there, matey?' 'Matey!' The friendliness of it, the – the – Just to prove how happy she was, just to show the tall fellow how at home she felt, and how she despised stupid conventions, Laura took a big bite of her bread-and-butter as she stared at the little drawing. She felt just like a work-girl.

'Laura, Laura, where are you? Telephone, Laura!' a voice cried from the house.

'Coming!' Away she skimmed, over the lawn, up the path, up the steps, across the veranda and into the porch. In the hall her father and Laurie were brushing their hats ready to go to the office.

'I say, Laura,' said Laurie very fast, 'you might just give a squiz at my coat before this afternoon. See if it wants pressing.'

'I will,' said she. Suddenly she couldn't stop herself. She ran at Laurie and gave him a small, quick squeeze. 'Oh, I do love parties, don't you?' gasped Laura.

'Ra-ther,' said Laurie's warm, boyish voice, and he squeezed his sister too and gave her a gentle push. 'Dash off to the telephone, old girl.'

The telephone. 'Yes, yes; oh yes. Kitty? Good morning, dear. Come to lunch? Do, dear. Delighted, of course. It will only be a very scratch meal – just the sandwich crusts and broken meringue-shells and what's left over. Yes, isn't it a perfect morning? Your white? Oh, I certainly should. One moment – hold the line. Mother's calling.' And Laura sat back. 'What, mother? Can't hear.'

Mrs Sheridan's voice floated down the stairs. 'Tell her to wear that sweet hat she had on last Sunday.'

'Mother says you're to wear that *sweet* hat you had on last Sunday. Good. One o'clock. Bye-bye.'

Laura put back the receiver, flung her arms over her head, took a deep breath, stretched and let them fall. 'Huh,' she sighed, and the moment after the sigh she sat up quickly. She was still, listening. All the doors in the house seemed to be open. The house was alive with soft, quick steps and running voices. The green baize door that led to the kitchen regions swung open and shut with a muffled thud. And now there came a long, chuckling absurd sound. It was the heavy piano being moved on its stiff castors. But the air! If you stopped to notice, was the air always like this? Little faint winds were playing chase in at the tops of the windows, out at the doors. And there were two tiny spots of sun, one on the inkpot, one 43 on a silver photograph frame, playing too. Darling little spots. Especially the one on the inkpot lid. It was quite warm. A warm little silver star. She could have kissed it.

The front door bell pealed and there sounded the rustle of Sadie's print skirt on the stairs. A man's voice murmured; Sadie answered, careless, 'I'm sure I don't know. Wait. I'll ask Mrs Sheridan.'

'What is it, Sadie?' Laura came into the hall.

'It's the florist, Miss Laura.'

It was, indeed. There, just inside the door, stood a wide, shallow tray full of pots of pink lilies. No other kind. Nothing but lilies — canna lilies, big pink flowers, wide open, radiant, almost frighteningly alive on bright crimson stems.

'O-oh, Sadie!' said Laura, and the sound was like a little moan. She crouched down as if to warm herself at that blaze of lilies; she felt they were in her fingers, on her lips, growing in her breast.

'It's some mistake,' she said faintly. 'Nobody ever ordered so many. Sadie, go and find mother.'

But at that moment Mrs Sheridan joined them.

'It's quite right,' she said calmly. 'Yes, I ordered them. Aren't they lovely?' She pressed Laura's arm. 'I was passing the shop yesterday, and I saw them in the window. And I suddenly thought for once in my life I shall have enough canna lilies. The garden-party will be a good excuse.'

'But I thought you said you didn't mean to interfere,' said Laura. Sadie had gone. The florist's man was still outside at his van. She put her arm round her mother's neck and 44 gently, very gently, she bit her mother's ear.

'My darling child, you wouldn't like a logical mother, would you? Don't do that. Here's the man.'

He carried more lilies still, another whole tray.

'Bank them up, just inside the door, on both sides of the porch, please,' said Mrs. Sheridan. 'Don't you agree, Laura?'

'Oh, I *do*, mother.'

In the drawing-room Meg, Jose and good little Hans had at last succeeded in moving the piano.

'Now, if we put this chesterfield against the wall and move everything out of the room except the chairs, don't you think?'

'Quite.'

'Hans, move these tables into the smoking-room, and bring a sweeper to take these marks off the carpet and – one moment, Hans –' Jose loved giving orders to the servants and they loved obeying her. She always made them feel they were taking part in some drama. 'Tell mother and Miss Laura to come here at once.'

'Very good, Miss Jose.'

She turned to Meg. 'I want to hear what the piano sounds like, just in case I'm asked to sing this afternoon. Let's try over "This Life is Weary".'

Pom! Ta-ta-ta *Tee*-ta! The piano burst out so passionately that Jose's face changed. She clasped her hands. She looked mournfully and enigmatically at her mother and Laura as they came in.

This Life is *Wee*-ary,
A Tear – a Sigh.

45

> A Love that *Chan*-ges,
>   This Life is *Wee*-ary,
> A Tear – a Sigh.
> A Love that *Chan*-ges,
> And then . . . Good-bye!

But at the word 'Good-bye', and although the piano sounded more desperate than ever, her face broke into a brilliant, dreadfully unsympathetic smile.

'Aren't I in good voice, mummy?' she beamed.

> This Life is *Wee*-ary,
> Hope comes to Die.
> A Dream – a *Wa*-kening.

But now Sadie interrupted them. 'What is it, Sadie?'

'If you please m'm, cook says have you got the flags for sandwiches?'

'The flags for the sandwiches, Sadie?' echoed Mrs Sheridan dreamily. And the children knew by her face that she hadn't got them. 'Let me see.' And she said to Sadie firmly, 'Tell cook I'll let her have them in ten minutes.'

Sadie went.

'Now, Laura,' said her mother quickly, 'come with me into the smoking-room. I've got the names somewhere on the back of an envelope. You'll have to write them out for me. Meg, go upstairs this minute and take that wet thing off your head. Jose, run and finish dressing this instant. Do you hear me, children, or shall I have to tell your father when he comes home tonight? And – and, Jose, pacify cook if you do go into the kitchen, will you? I'm terrified of her this morning.'

The envelope was found at last behind the dining-room clock, though how it had got there Mrs Sheridan could not imagine.

'One of you children must have stolen it out of my bag, because I remember vividly – cream-cheese and lemon-curd. Have you done that?'

'Yes.'

'Egg and –' Mrs Sheridan held the envelope away from her. 'It looks like mice. It can't be mice, can it?'

'Olive, pet,' said Laura, looking over her shoulder.

'Yes, of course, olive. What a horrible combination it sounds. Egg and olive.'

They were finished at last, and Laura took them off to the kitchen. She found Jose there pacifying the cook, who did not look at all terrifying.

'I have never seen such exquisite sandwiches,' said Jose's voice. 'How many kinds did you say there were, cook? Fifteen?'

'Fifteen, Miss Jose.'

'Well, cook, I congratulate you.'

Cook swept up crusts with the long sandwich knife, and smiled broadly.

'Godber's has come,' announced Sadie, issuing out of the pantry. She had seen the man pass the window.

That meant the cream puffs had come. Godber's were famous for their cream puffs. Nobody ever thought of making them at home.

'Bring them in and put them on the table, my girl,' ordered cook.

Sadie brought them in and went back to the door. Of course Laura and Jose were far too grown-up to really care about such things. All the same, they couldn't help agreeing that the puffs looked very attractive. Very. Cook began arranging them, shaking off the extra icing sugar.

'Don't they carry one back to all one's parties?' said Laura.

'I suppose they do,' said practical Jose, who never liked to be carried back. 'They look beautifully light and feathery, I must say.'

'Have one each, my dears,' said cook in her comfortable voice. 'Yer ma won't know.'

Oh, impossible. Fancy cream puffs so soon after breakfast. The very idea made one shudder. All the same, two minutes later Jose and Laura were licking their fingers with that absorbed inward look that only comes from whipped cream.

'Let's go into the garden, out by the back way,' suggested Laura. 'I want to see how the men are getting on with the marquee. They're such awfully nice men.'

But the back door was blocked by cook, Sadie, Godber's man and Hans.

Something had happened.

'Tuk-tuk-tuk,' clucked cook like an agitated hen. Sadie had her hand clapped to her cheek as though she had toothache. Hans's face was screwed up in the effort to understand. Only Godber's man seemed to be enjoying himself; it was his story.

'What's the matter? What's happened?'

'There's been a horrible accident,' said cook. 'A man killed.'

48

'A man killed! Where? How? When?'

But Godber's man wasn't going to have his story snatched from under his very nose.

'Know those little cottages just below here, miss?' Know them? Of course she knew them. 'Well, there's a young chap living there, name of Scott, a carter. His horse shied at a traction-engine, corner of Hawke Street this morning, and he was thrown out on the back of his head. Killed.'

'Dead!' Laura stared at Godber's man.

'Dead when they picked him up,' said Godber's man with relish. 'They were taking the body home as I come up here.' And he said to the cook, 'He's left a wife and five little ones.'

'Jose, come here.' Laura caught hold of her sister's sleeve and dragged her through the kitchen to the other side of the green baize door. There she paused and leaned against it. 'Jose!' she said, horrified, 'However are we going to stop everything?'

'Stop everything, Laura!' cried Jose in astonishment. 'What do you mean?'

'Stop the garden-party, of course.' Why did Jose pretend? But Jose was still more amazed. 'Stop the garden-party? My dear Laura, don't be so absurd. Of course we can't do anything of the kind. Nobody expects us to. Don't be so extravagant.'

'But we can't possibly have a garden-party with a man dead just outside the front gate.'

That really was extravagant, for the little cottages were in a lane to themselves at the very bottom of a steep rise that led up to the house. A broad road ran between. True, they were far too near. They were the greatest possible eyesore and they had no right to be in that neighbourhood at all. They were little mean dwellings painted a chocolate brown. In the garden patches there was nothing but cabbage stalks, sick hens and tomato cans. The very smoke coming out of their chimneys was poverty-stricken. Little rags and shreds of smoke, so unlike the great silvery plumes that uncurled from the Sheridans' chimneys. Washerwomen lived in the lane and sweeps and a cobbler and a man whose house-front was studded all over with minute bird-cages. Children swarmed. When the Sheridans were little they were forbidden to set foot there because of the revolting language and of what they might catch. But since they were grown up Laura and Laurie on their prowls sometimes walked through. It was disgusting and sordid. They came out with a shudder. But still one must go everywhere; one must see everything. So through they went.

'And just think of what the band would sound like to that poor woman,' said Laura.

'Oh, Laura!' Jose began to be seriously annoyed. 'If you're going to stop a band playing every time someone has an accident, you'll lead a very strenuous life. I'm every bit as sorry about it as you. I feel just as sympathetic.' Her eyes hardened. She looked at her sister just as she used to when they were little and fighting together. 'You won't bring a drunken workman back to life by being sentimental,' she said softly.

50   'Drunk! Who said he was drunk?' Laura turned furiously

on Jose. She said just as they had used to say on those occasions, 'I'm going straight up to tell mother.'

'Do, dear,' cooed Jose.

'Mother, can I come into your room?' Laura turned the big glass door-knob.

'Of course, child. Why, what's the matter? What's given you such a colour?' And Mrs Sheridan turned round from her dressing-table. She was trying on a new hat.

'Mother, a man's been killed,' began Laura.

'*Not* in the garden?' interrupted her mother.

'No, no!'

'Oh, what a fright you gave me!' Mrs Sheridan sighed with relief and took off the big hat and held it on her knees.

'But listen, mother,' said Laura. Breathless, half choking, she told the dreadful story. 'Of course, we can't have our party, can we?' she pleaded. 'The band and everybody arriving. They'd hear us, mother; they're nearly neighbours!'

To Laura's astonishment her mother behaved just like Jose; it was harder to bear because she seemed amused. She refused to take Laura seriously.

'But, my dear child, use your common sense. It's only by accident we've heard of it. If someone had died there normally – and I can't understand how they keep alive in those poky little holes – we should still be having our party, shouldn't we?'

Laura had to say 'yes' to that, but she felt it was all wrong. She sat down on her mother's sofa and pinched the cushion frill.

'Mother, isn't it really terribly heartless of us?' she asked.

'Darling!' Mrs Sheridan got up and came over to her, carrying the hat. Before Laura could stop her she had popped it on. 'My child!' said her mother, 'the hat is yours. It's made for you. It's much too young for me. I have never seen you look such a picture. Look at yourself!' And she held up her hand-mirror.

'But, mother,' Laura began again. She couldn't look at herself; she turned aside.

This time Mrs Sheridan lost patience just as Jose had done.

'You are being very absurd, Laura,' she said coldly. 'People like that don't expect sacrifices from us. And it's not very sympathetic to spoil everybody's enjoyment as you're doing now.'

'I don't understand,' said Laura, and she walked quickly out of the room into her own bedroom. There, quite by chance, the first thing she saw was this charming girl in the mirror, in her black hat trimmed with gold daisies and a long black velvet ribbon. Never had she imagined she could look like that. Is mother right? she thought. And now she hoped her mother was right. Am I being extravagant? Perhaps it was extravagant. Just for a moment she had another glimpse of that poor woman and those little children and the body being carried into the house. But it all seemed blurred, unreal, like a picture in the newspaper. I'll remember it again, after the party's over, she decided. And somehow that seemed quite the best plan . . .

Lunch was over by half-past one. By half-past two they

were all ready for the fray. The green-coated band had arrived and was established in a corner of the tennis-court.

'My dear!' trilled Kitty Maitland, 'aren't they too like frogs for words? You ought to have arranged them round the pond with the conductor in the middle on a leaf.'

Laurie arrived and hailed them on his way to dress. At the sight of him Laura remembered the accident again. She wanted to tell him. If Laurie agreed with the others, then it was bound to be all right. And she followed him into the hall.

'Laurie!'

'Hallo!' He was half-way upstairs, but when he turned round and saw Laura he suddenly puffed out his cheeks and goggled his eyes at her. 'My word, Laura! You do look stunning,' said Laurie. 'What an absolutely topping hat!'

Laura said faintly, 'Is it?' and smiled up at Laurie and didn't tell him after all.

Soon after that people began coming in streams. The band struck up; the hired waiters ran from the house to the marquee. Wherever you looked there were couples strolling, bending to the flowers, greeting, moving on over the lawn. They were like bright birds that had alighted in the Sheridans' garden for this one afternoon, on their way to – where? Ah, what happiness it is to be with people who all are happy, to press hands, press cheeks, smile into eyes.

'Darling Laura, how well you look!'

'What a becoming hat, child!'

'Laura, you look quite Spanish. I've never seen you look so striking.'

And Laura, glowing, answered softly, 'Have you had tea?

Won't you have an ice? The passion-fruit ices really are rather special.' She ran to her father and begged him: 'Daddy darling, can't the band have something to drink?'

And the perfect afternoon slowly ripened, slowly faded, slowly its petals closed.

'Never a more delightful garden-party . . .' 'The greatest success . . .' 'Quite the most . . .'

Laura helped her mother with the good-byes. They stood side by side in the porch till it was all over.

'All over, all over, thank heaven,' said Mrs Sheridan. 'Round up the others, Laura. Let's go and have some fresh coffee. I'm exhausted. Yes, it's been very successful. But oh, these parties, these parties! Why will you children insist on giving parties!' And they all of them sat down in the deserted marquee.

'Have a sandwich, daddy dear. I wrote the flag.'

'Thanks.' Mr Sheridan took a bite and the sandwich was gone. He took another. 'I suppose you didn't hear of a beastly accident that happened today?' he said.

'My dear,' said Mrs Sheridan, holding up her hand, 'we did. It nearly ruined the party. Laura insisted we should put it off.'

'Oh, mother!' Laura didn't want to be teased about it.

'It was a horrible affair all the same,' said Mr Sheridan. 'The chap was married too. Lived just below in the lane, and leaves a wife and half a dozen kiddies, so they say.'

An awkward little silence fell. Mrs Sheridan fidgeted with her cup. Really, it was very tactless of father . . .

Suddenly she looked up. There on the table were all those

sandwiches, cakes, puffs, all uneaten, all going to be wasted. She had one of her brilliant ideas.

'I know,' she said. 'Let's make up a basket. Let's send that poor creature some of this perfectly good food. At any rate, it will be the greatest treat for the children. Don't you agree? And she's sure to have neighbours calling in and so on. What a point to have it all ready prepared. Laura!' She jumped up. 'Get me the big basket out of the stairs cupboard.'

'But, mother, do you really think it's a good idea?' said Laura.

Again, how curious, she seemed to be different from them all. To take scraps from their party. Would the poor woman really like that?

'Of course! What's the matter with you today? An hour or two ago you were insisting on us being sympathetic.'

Oh well! Laura ran for the basket. It was filled, it was now heaped by her mother.

'Take it yourself, darling,' said she. 'Run down just as you are. No, wait, take the arum lilies too. People of that class are so impressed by arum lilies.'

'The stems will ruin her lace frock,' said practical Jose.

So they would. Just in time. 'Only the basket, then. And, Laura!' – her mother followed her out of the marquee – 'don't on any account –'

'What, mother?'

No, better not put such ideas into the child's head! 'Nothing! Run along.'

It was just growing dusky as Laura shut their garden 55

gates. A big dog ran by like a shadow. The road gleamed white, and down below in the hollow the little cottages were in deep shade. How quiet it seemed after the afternoon. Here she was going down the hill to somewhere where a man lay dead, and she couldn't realize it. Why couldn't she? She stopped a minute. And it seemed to her that kisses, voices, tinkling spoons, laughter, the smell of crushed grass were somehow inside her. She had no room for anything else. How strange! She looked up at the pale sky, and all she thought was, 'Yes, it was the most successful party.'

Now the broad road was crossed. The lane began, smoky and dark. Women in shawls and men's tweed caps hurried by. Men hung over the palings; the children played in the doorways. A low hum came from the mean little cottages. In some of them there was a flicker of light, and a shadow, crab-like, moved across the window. Laura bent her head and hurried on. She wished now she had put on a coat. How her frock shone! And the big hat with the velvet streamer – if only it was another hat! Were the people looking at her? They must be. It was a mistake to have come; she knew all along it was a mistake. Should she go back even now?

No, too late. This was the house. It must be. A dark knot of people stood outside. Beside the gate an old, old woman with a crutch sat in a chair, watching. She had her feet on a newspaper. The voices stopped as Laura drew near. The group parted. It was as though she was expected, as though they had known she was coming here.

Laura was terribly nervous. Tossing the velvet ribbon over her shoulder, she said to a woman standing by, 'Is this Mrs

Scott's house?' and the woman, smiling queerly, said, 'It is, my lass.'

Oh, to be away from this! She actually said, 'Help me, God,' as she walked up the tiny path and knocked. To be away from those staring eyes, or to be covered up in anything, one of those women's shawls even. I'll just leave the basket and go, she decided. I shan't even wait for it to be emptied.

Then the door opened. A little woman in black showed in the gloom.

Laura said, 'Are you Mrs Scott?' But to her horror the woman answered, 'Walk in, please, miss,' and she was shut in the passage.

'No,' said Laura, 'I don't want to come in. I only want to leave this basket. Mother sent –'

The little woman in the gloomy passage seemed not to have heard her. 'Step this way, please, miss,' she said in an oily voice, and Laura followed her.

She found herself in a wretched little low kitchen, lighted by a smoky lamp. There was a woman sitting before the fire.

'Em,' said the little creature who had let her in. 'Em! It's a young lady.' She turned to Laura. She said meaningly, 'I'm 'er sister, miss. You'll excuse 'er, won't you?'

'Oh, but of course!' said Laura. 'Please, please don't disturb her. I – I only want to leave –'

But at that moment the woman at the fire turned round. Her, face, puffed up, red, with swollen eyes and swollen lips, looked terrible. She seemed as though she couldn't under-stand why Laura was there. What did it mean? Why was this stranger standing in the kitchen with a basket? What was it all about? And the poor face puckered up again.

'All right, my dear,' said the other. 'I'll thenk the young lady.'

And again she began, 'You'll excuse her, miss, I'm sure,' and her face, swollen too, tried an oily smile.

Laura only wanted to get out, to get away. She was back in the passage. The door opened. She walked straight through into the bedroom, where the dead man was lying.

'You'd like a look at 'im, wouldn't you?' said Em's sister, and she brushed past Laura over to the bed. 'Don't be afraid, my lass' – and now her voice sounded fond and sly, and fondly she drew down the sheet – ''e looks a picture. There's nothing to show. Come along, my dear.'

Laura came.

There lay a young man, fast asleep – sleeping so soundly, so deeply, that he was far, far away from them both. Oh, so remote, so peaceful. He was dreaming. Never wake him up again. His head was sunk in the pillow, his eyes were closed; they were blind under the closed eyelids. He was given up to his dream. What did garden-parties and baskets and lace frocks matter to him? He was far from all those things. He was wonderful, beautiful. While they were laughing and while the band was playing, this marvel had come to the lane. Happy . . . happy . . . All is well, said that sleeping face. This is just as it should be. I am content.

But all the same you had to cry, and she couldn't go out of the room without saying something to him. Laura gave a loud childish sob.

'Forgive my hat,' she said.

And this time she didn't wait for Em's sister. She found her way out of the door, down the path past all those dark people. At the corner of the lane she met Laurie.

He stepped out of the shadow. 'Is that you, Laura?'

'Yes.'

'Mother was getting anxious. Was it all right?'

'Yes, quite, Oh, Laurie!' She took his arm, she pressed up against him.

'I say, you're not crying, are you?' asked her brother.

Laura shook her head. She was.

Laurie put his arm round her shoulder. 'Don't cry,' he said in his warm, loving voice. 'Was it awful?'

'No,' sobbed Laura. 'It was simply marvellous. But, Laurie –' She stopped, she looked at her brother. 'Isn't life,' she stammered, 'isn't life –' But what life was she couldn't explain. No matter. He quite understood.

'*Isn't* it, darling?' said Laurie.

Bliss

Although Bertha Young was thirty she still had moments like this when she wanted to run instead of walk, to take dancing steps on and off the pavement, to bowl a hoop, to throw something up in the air and catch it again, or to stand still and laugh at – nothing – at nothing, simply.

What can you do if you are thirty and, turning the corner of your own street, you are overcome, suddenly, by a feeling of bliss – absolute bliss! – as though you'd suddenly swallowed a bright piece of that late afternoon sun and it burned in your bosom, sending out a little shower of sparks into every particle, into every finger and toe? . . .

Oh, is there no way you can express it without being 'drunk and disorderly'? How idiotic civilization is! Why be given a body if you have to keep it shut up in a case like a rare, rare fiddle?

'No, that about the fiddle is not quite what I mean,' she thought, running up the steps and feeling in her bag for the key – she'd forgotten it, as usual – and rattling the letter-box. 'It's not what I mean, because – Thank you, Mary' – she went into the hall. 'Is nurse back?'

'Yes, m'm.'

'And has the fruit come?'

'Yes, m'm. Everything's come.'

'Bring the fruit up to the dining-room, will you? I'll arrange it before I go upstairs.'

It was dusky in the dining-room and quite chilly. But all the same Bertha threw off her coat; she could not bear the tight clasp of it another moment, and the cold air fell on her arms.

But in her bosom there was still that bright glowing place – that shower of little sparks coming from it. It was almost unbearable. She hardly dared to breathe for fear of fanning it higher, and yet she breathed deeply, deeply. She hardly dared to look into the cold mirror – but she did look, and it gave her back a woman, radiant, with smiling, trembling lips, with big, dark eyes and an air of listening, waiting for something . . . divine to happen . . . that she knew must happen . . . infallibly.

Mary brought in the fruit, on a tray and with it a glass bowl, and a blue dish, very lovely, with a strange sheen on it as though it had been dipped in milk.

'Shall I turn on the light, m'm?'

'No, thank you. I can see quite well.'

There were tangerines and apples stained with strawberry pink. Some yellow pears, smooth as silk, some white grapes covered with a silver bloom and a big cluster of purple ones. These last she had bought to tone in with the new dining-room carpet. Yes, that did sound rather far-fetched and absurd, but it was really why she had bought them. She had thought in the shop: 'I must have some purple ones to bring the carpet up to the table.' And it had seemed quite sense at the time.

When she had finished with them and had made two

pyramids of these bright round shapes, she stood away from the table to get the effect – and it really was most curious. For the dark table seemed to melt into the dusky light and the glass dish and the blue bowl to float in the air. This, of course, in her present mood, was so incredibly beautiful . . . She began to laugh.

'No, no. I'm getting hysterical.' And she seized her bag and coat and ran upstairs to the nursery.

Nurse sat at a low table giving Little B her supper after her bath. The baby had on a white flannel gown and a blue woollen jacket, and her dark, fine hair was brushed up into a funny little peak. She looked up when she saw her mother and began to jump.

'Now, my lovey, eat it up like a good girl,' said nurse, setting her lips in a way that Bertha knew, and that meant she had come into the nursery at another wrong moment.

'Has she been good, Nanny?'

'She's been a little sweet all the afternoon,' whispered Nanny. 'We went to the park and I sat down on a chair and took her out of the pram and a big dog came along and put its head on my knee and she clutched its ear, tugged it. Oh, you should have seen her.'

Bertha wanted to ask if it wasn't rather dangerous to let her clutch at a strange dog's ear. But she did not dare to. She stood watching them, her hands by her side, like the poor little girl in front of the rich little girl with the doll.

The baby looked up at her again, stared, and then smiled so charmingly that Bertha couldn't help crying:

'Oh, Nanny, do let me finish giving her her supper while you put the bath things away.'

'Well, m'm, she oughtn't to be changed hands while she's eating,' said Nanny, still whispering. 'It unsettles her; it's very likely to upset her.'

How absurd it was. Why have a baby if it has to be kept – not in a case like a rare, rare fiddle – but in another woman's arms?

'Oh, I must!' said she.

Very offended, Nanny handed her over.

'Now, don't excite her after her supper. You know you do, m'm. And I have such a time with her after!'

Thank heaven! Nanny went out of the room with the bath towels.

'Now I've got you to myself, my little precious,' said Bertha, as the baby leaned against her.

She ate delightfully, holding up her lips for the spoon and then waving her hands. Sometimes she wouldn't let the spoon go; and sometimes, just as Bertha had filled it, she waved it away to the four winds.

When the soup was finished Bertha turned round to the fire.

'You're nice – you're very nice!' said she, kissing her warm baby. 'I'm fond of you. I like you.'

And, indeed, she loved Little B so much – her neck as she bent forward, her exquisite toes as they shone transparent in the firelight – that all her feeling of bliss came back again, and again she didn't know how to express it – what to do with it.

'You're wanted on the telephone,' said Nanny, coming back in triumph and seizing *her* Little B.

Down she flew. It was Harry.

'Oh, is that you, Ber? Look here. I'll be late. I'll take a taxi and come along as quickly as I can, but get dinner put back ten minutes – will you? All right?'

'Yes, perfectly. Oh, Harry!'

'Yes?'

What had she to say? She'd nothing to say. She only wanted to get in touch with him for a moment. She couldn't absurdly cry: 'Hasn't it been a divine day!'

'What is it?' rapped out the little voice.

'Nothing. *Entendu*,' said Bertha, and hung up the receiver, thinking how much more than idiotic civilization was.

They had people coming to dinner. The Norman Knights – a very sound couple – he was about to start a theatre, and she was awfully keen on interior decoration, a young man, Eddie Warren, who had just published a little book of poems and whom everybody was asking to dine, and a 'find' of Bertha's called Pearl Fulton. What Miss Fulton did, Bertha didn't know. They had met at the club and Bertha had fallen in love with her, as she always did fall in love with beautiful women who had something strange about them.

The provoking thing was that, though they had been about together and met a number of times and really talked, Bertha couldn't make her out. Up to a certain point Miss Fulton was rarely, wonderfully frank, but the certain point was there, and beyond that she would not go.

Was there anything beyond it? Harry said 'No.' Voted her dullish, and 'cold like all blonde women, with a touch, perhaps, of anæmia of the brain'. But Bertha wouldn't agree with him; not yet, at any rate.

'No, the way she has of sitting with her head a little on one side, and smiling, has something behind it, Harry, and I must find out what that something is.'

'Most likely it's a good stomach,' answered Harry.

He made a point of catching Bertha's heels with replies of that kind . . . 'liver frozen, my dear girl', 'pure flatulence', or 'kidney disease', . . . and so on. For some strange reason Bertha liked this, and almost admired it in him very much.

She went into the drawing-room and lighted the fire; then, picking up the cushions, one by one, that Mary had disposed so carefully, she threw them back on to the chairs and the couches. That made all the difference; the room came alive at once. As she was about to throw the last one she surprised herself by suddenly hugging it to her, passionately, passionately. But it did not put out the fire in her bosom. Oh, on the contrary!

The windows of the drawing-room opened on to a balcony overlooking the garden. At the far end, against the wall, there was a tall, slender pear tree in fullest, richest bloom; it stood perfect, as though becalmed against the jade-green sky. Bertha couldn't help feeling, even from this distance, that it had not a single bud or a faded petal. Down below, in the garden beds, the red and yellow tulips, heavy with flowers, seemed to lean upon the dusk. A grey cat, dragging its belly, crept across the lawn, and a black one, its shadow, trailed after. The sight of them, so intent and so quick, gave Bertha a curious shiver.

'What creepy things cats are!' she stammered, and she turned away from the window and began walking up and down . . .

How strong the jonquils smelled in the warm room. Too strong? Oh, no. And yet, as though overcome, she flung down on a couch and pressed her hands to her eyes.

'I'm too happy – too happy!' she murmured.

And she seemed to see on her eyelids the lovely pear tree with its wide open blossoms as a symbol of her own life.

Really – really – she had everything. She was young. Harry and she were as much in love as ever, and they got on together splendidly and were really good pals. She had an adorable baby. They didn't have to worry about money. They had this absolutely satisfactory house and garden. And friends – modern, thrilling friends, writers and painters and poets or people keen on social questions – just the kind of friends they wanted. And then there were books, and there was music, and she had found a wonderful little dressmaker, and they were going abroad in the summer, and their new cook made the most superb omelettes . . .

'I'm absurd. Absurd!' She sat up; but she felt quite dizzy, quite drunk. It must have been the spring.

Yes, it was the spring. Now she was so tired she could not drag herself upstairs to dress.

A white dress, a string of jade beads, green shoes and stockings. It wasn't unintentional. She had thought of this scheme hours before she stood at the drawing-room window.

Her petals rustled softly into the hall, and she kissed Mrs Norman Knight, who was taking off the most amusing orange coat with a procession of black monkeys round the hem and up the fronts.

'. . . Why! Why! Why is the middle-class so stodgy – so utterly without a sense of humour! My dear, it's only by a fluke that I am here at all – Norman being the protective fluke. For my darling monkeys so upset the train that it rose to a man and simply ate me with its eyes. Didn't laugh – wasn't amused – that I should have loved. No, just stared – and bored me through and through.'

'But the cream of it was,' said Norman, pressing a large tortoiseshell-rimmed monocle into his eye, 'you don't mind me telling this, Face, do you?' (In their home and among their friends they called each other Face and Mug.) 'The cream of it was when she, being full fed, turned to the woman beside her and said: "Haven't you ever seen a monkey before?"'

'Oh yes!' Mrs Norman Knight joined in the laughter. 'Wasn't that too absolutely creamy?'

And a funnier thing still was that now her coat was off she did look like a very intelligent monkey – who had even made that yellow silk dress out of scraped banana skins. And her amber ear-rings: they were like little dangling nuts.

'This is a sad, sad fall!' said Mug, pausing in front of

Little B's perambulator. 'When the perambulator comes into the hall –' and he waved the rest of the quotation away.

The bell rang. It was lean, pale Eddie Warren (as usual) in a state of acute distress.

'It *is* the right house, *isn't* it?' he pleaded.

'Oh, I think so – I hope so,' said Bertha brightly.

'I have had such a *dreadful* experience with a taxi-man; he was *most* sinister. I couldn't get him to *stop*. The *more* I knocked and called the *faster* he went. And *in* the moonlight this *bizarre* figure with the *flattened* head *crouching* over the *lit-tle* wheel . . .'

He shuddered, taking off an immense white silk scarf. Bertha noticed that his socks were white, too – most charming.

'But how dreadful!' she cried.

'Yes, it really was,' said Eddie, following her into the drawing-room. 'I saw myself *driving* through Eternity in a *timeless* taxi.'

He knew the Norman Knights. In fact, he was going to write a play for N. K. when the theatre scheme came off.

'Well, Warren, how's the play?' said Norman Knight, dropping his monocle and giving his eye a moment in which to rise to the surface before it was screwed down again.

And Mrs Norman Knight: 'Oh, Mr Warren, what happy socks!'

'I *am* so glad you like them,' said he, staring at his feet. 'They seem to have got so *much* whiter since the moon rose.' And he turned his lean sorrowful young face to Bertha. 'There *is* a moon, you know.'

She wanted to cry: 'I am sure there is – often – often!'

He really was a most attractive person. But so was Face, crouched before the fire in her banana skins, and so was Mug, smoking a cigarette and saying as he flicked the ash: 'Why doth the bridegroom tarry?'

'There he is, now.'

Bang went the front door open and shut. Harry shouted: 'Hullo, you people. Down in five minutes.' And they heard him swarm up the stairs. Bertha couldn't help smiling; she knew how he loved doing things at high pressure. What, after all, did an extra five minutes matter? But he would pretend to himself that they mattered beyond measure. And then he would make a great point of coming into the drawing-room, extravagantly cool and collected.

Harry had such a zest for life. Oh, how she appreciated it in him. And his passion for fighting – for seeking in everything that came up against him another test of his power and of his courage – that, too, she understood. Even when it made him just occasionally, to other people, who didn't know him well, a little ridiculous perhaps ... For there were moments when he rushed into battle where no battle was ... She talked and laughed and positively forgot until he had come in (just as she had imagined) that Pearl Fulton had not turned up.

'I wonder if Miss Fulton has forgotten?'

'I expect so,' said Harry. 'Is she on the 'phone?'

'Ah! There's a taxi now.' And Bertha smiled with that little air of proprietorship that she always assumed while her women finds were new and mysterious. 'She lives in taxis.' 69

'She'll run to fat if she does,' said Harry coolly, ringing the bell for dinner. 'Frightful danger for blonde women.'

'Harry – don't,' warned Bertha, laughing up at him.

Came another tiny moment, while they waited, laughing and talking, just a trifle too much at their ease, a trifle too unaware. And then Miss Fulton, all in silver, with a silver fillet binding her pale blonde hair, came in smiling, her head a little on one side.

'Am I late?'

'No, not at all,' said Bertha. 'Come along.' And she took her arm and they moved into the dining-room.

What was there in the touch of that cool arm that could fan – fan – start blazing – blazing – the fire of bliss that Bertha did not know what to do with?

Miss Fulton did not look at her; but then she seldom did look at people directly. Her heavy eyelids lay upon her eyes and the strange half-smile came and went upon her lips as though she lived by listening rather than seeing. But Bertha knew, suddenly, as if the longest, most intimate look had passed between them — as if they had said to each other: 'You, too?' – that Pearl Fulton, stirring the beautiful red soup in the grey plate, was feeling just what she was feeling.

And the others? Face and Mug, Eddie and Harry, their spoons rising and falling – dabbing their lips with their napkins, crumbling bread, fiddling with the forks and glasses and talking.

'I met her at the Alpha show – the weirdest little person. She'd not only cut off her hair, but she seemed to have taken

70

a dreadfully good snip off her legs and arms and her neck and her poor little nose as well.'

'Isn't she very *liée* with Michael Oat?'

'The man who wrote *Love in False Teeth*?'

'He wants to write a play for me. One act. One man. Decides to commit suicide. Gives all the reasons why he should and why he shouldn't. And just as he has made up his mind either to do it or not to do it – curtain. Not half a bad idea.'

'What's he going to call it – *Stomach Trouble*?'

'I *think* I've come across the *same* idea in a lit–tle French review, *quite* unknown in England.'

No, they didn't share it. They were dears – dears – and she loved having them there, at her table, and giving them delicious food and wine. In fact, she longed to tell them how delightful they were, and what a decorative group they made, how they seemed to set one another off and how they reminded her of a play by Tchekof!

Harry was enjoying his dinner. It was part of his – well, not his nature, exactly, and certainly not his pose – his – something or other – to talk about food and to glory in his 'shameless passion for the white flesh of the lobster' and 'the green of pistachio ices – green and cold like the eyelids of Egyptian dancers'.

When he looked up at her and said: 'Bertha, this is a very admirable *soufflé*!' she almost could have wept with child-like pleasure.

Oh, why did she feel so tender towards the whole world tonight? Everything was good – was right. All that happened seemed to fill again her brimming cup of bliss.

And still, in the back of her mind, there was the pear tree. It would be silver now, in the light of poor dear Eddie's moon, silver as Miss Fulton, who sat there turning a tangerine in her slender fingers that were so pale a light seemed to come from them.

What she simply couldn't make out – what was miraculous – was how she should have guessed Miss Fulton's mood so exactly and so instantly. For she never doubted for a moment that she was right, and yet what had she to go on? Less than nothing.

'I believe this does happen very, very rarely between women. Never between men,' thought Bertha. 'But while I am making the coffee in the drawing-room perhaps she will "give a sign".'

What she meant by that she did not know, and what would happen after that she could not imagine.

While she thought like this she saw herself talking and laughing. She had to talk because of her desire to laugh.

'I must laugh or die.'

But when she noticed Face's funny little habit of tucking something down the front of her bodice – as if she kept a tiny, secret hoard of nuts there, too – Bertha had to dig her nails into her hands – so as not to laugh too much.

It was over at last. And: 'Come and see my new coffee machine,' said Bertha.

'We only have a new coffee machine once a fortnight,' Harry. Face took her arm this time; Miss Fulton bent her head and followed after.

The fire had died down in the drawing-room to a red, flickering 'nest of baby phœnixes', said Face.

'Don't turn up the light for a moment. It is so lovely.' And down she crouched by the fire again. She was always cold . . . 'without her little red flannel jacket, of course,' thought Bertha.

At that moment Miss Fulton 'gave the sign'.

'Have you a garden?' said the cool, sleepy voice.

This was so exquisite on her part that all Bertha could do was to obey. She crossed the room, pulled the curtains apart, and opened those long windows.

'There!' she breathed.

And the two women stood side by side looking at the slender, flowering tree. Although it was so still it seemed, like the flame of a candle, to stretch up, to point, to quiver in the bright air, to grow taller and taller as they gazed – almost to touch the rim of the round, silver moon.

How long did they stand there? Both, as it were, caught in that circle of unearthly light, understanding each other perfectly, creatures of another world, and wondering what they were to do in this one with all this blissful treasure that burned in their bosoms and dropped, in silver flowers, from their hair and hands?

For ever – for a moment? And did Miss Fulton murmur: 'Yes. Just *that*.' Or did Bertha dream it?

Then the light was snapped on and Face made the coffee and Harry said: 'My dear Mrs Knight, don't ask me about my baby. I never see her. I shan't feel the slightest interest in her until she has a lover,' and Mug took his eye out of the conservatory for a moment and then put it under glass again and Eddie Warren drank his coffee and set down the cup with a face of anguish as though he had drunk and seen the spider.

'What I want to do is to give the young men a show. I believe London is simply teeming with first-chop, unwritten plays. What I want to say to 'em is: "Here's the theatre. Fire ahead".'

'You know, my dear, I am going to decorate a room for the Jacob Nathans. Oh, I am so tempted to do a fried-fish scheme, with the backs of the chairs shaped like frying-pans and lovely chip potatoes embroidered all over the curtains.'

'The trouble with our young writing men is that they are still too romantic. You can't put out to sea without being seasick and wanting a basin. Well, why won't they have the courage of those basins?'

'A *dreadful* poem about a *girl* who was *violated* by a beggar *without* a nose in a lit-tIe wood . . .'

Miss Fulton sank into the lowest, deepest chair and Harry handed round the cigarettes.

From the way he stood in front of her shaking the silver box and saying abruptly: 'Egyptian? Turkish? Virginian? They're all mixed up,' Bertha realized that she not only bored him; he really disliked her. And she decided from the way Miss Fulton said: 'No, thank you, I won't smoke,' that she felt it, too, and was hurt.

'Oh, Harry, don't dislike her. You are quite wrong about her. She's wonderful, wonderful. And, besides, how can you

feel so differently about someone who means so much to me?
I shall try to tell you when we are in bed tonight what has
been happening. What she and I have shared.'

At those last words something strange and almost terrifying
darted into Bertha's mind. And this something blind and
smiling whispered to her: 'Soon these people will go. The
house will be quiet – quiet. The lights will be out. And you
and he will be alone together in the dark room – the warm
bed . . .'

She jumped up from her chair and ran over to the piano.

'What a pity someone does not play!' she cried. 'What a
pity somebody does not play.'

For the first time in her life Bertha Young desired her
husband.

Oh, she'd loved him – she'd been in love with him, of
course, in every other way, but just not in that way. And
equally, of course, she'd understood that he was different.
They'd discussed it so often. It had worried her dreadfully at
first to find that she was so cold, but after a time it had not
seemed to matter. They were so frank with each other – such
good pals. That was the best of being modern.

But now – ardently! Ardently! The word ached in her
ardent body! Was this what that feeling of bliss had been
leading up to? But then, then –

'My dear,' said Mr Norman Knight, 'you know our shame.
We are the victims of time and train. We live in Hampstead.
It's been so nice.'

'I'll come with you into the hall,' said Bertha. 'I loved

having you. But you must not miss the last train. That's so awful, isn't it.'

'Have a whisky, Knight, before you go?' called Harry.

'No, thanks, old chap.'

Bertha squeezed his hand for that as she shook it.

'Good night, goodbye,' she cried from the top step, feeling that this self of hers was taking leave of them for ever.

When she got back into the drawing-room the others were on the move.

'. . . Then you can come part of the way in my taxi.'

'I shall be *so* thankful not to have to face *another* drive *alone* after my *dreadful experience.*'

'You can get a taxi at the rank just at the end of the street. You won't have to walk more than a few yards.'

'That's a comfort. I'll go and put on my coat.'

Miss Fulton moved towards the hall and Bertha was following when Harry almost pushed past.

'Let me help you.'

Bertha knew that he was repenting his rudeness – she let him go. What a boy he was in some ways – so impulsive – so – simple.

And Eddie and she were left by the fire.

'I *wonder* if you have seen Bilks' *new* poem called "Table d'Hôte",' said Eddie softly. 'It's *so* wonderful. In the last Anthology. Have you got a copy? I'd *so* like to *show* it to you. It begins with an *incredibly* beautiful line: "Why must it always be tomato soup?"'

'Yes,' said Bertha. And she moved noiselessly to a table opposite the drawing-room door and Eddie glided noiselessly after her. She picked up the little book and gave it to him; they had not made a sound.

While he looked it up she turned her head towards the hall. And she saw ... Harry with Miss Fulton's coat in his arms and Miss Fulton with her back turned to him and her head bent. He tossed the coat away, put his hands on her shoulders and turned her violently to him. His lips said: 'I adore you,' and Miss Fulton laid her moonbeam fingers on his cheeks and smiled her sleepy smile. Harry's nostrils quivered; his lips curled back in a hideous grin while he whispered: 'Tomorrow,' and with her eyelids Miss Fulton said: 'Yes.'

'Here it is,' said Eddie. '"Why must it always be tomato soup?" It's so *deeply* true, don't you feel? Tomato soup is so *dreadfully* eternal.'

'If you prefer,' said Harry's voice, very loud, from the hall, I can 'phone you a cab to come to the door.'

'Oh, no. It's not necessary,' said Miss Fulton, and she came up to Bertha and gave her the slender fingers to hold.

'Goodbye. Thank you so much.'

'Goodbye,' said Bertha.

Miss Fulton held her hand a moment longer.

'Your lovely pear tree!' she murmured.

And then she was gone, with Eddie following, like the black cat following the grey cat.

'I'll shut up shop,' said Harry, extravagantly cool and collected.

'Your lovely pear tree – pear tree – pear tree!'

Bertha simply ran over to the long windows.

'Oh, what is going to happen now?' she cried.

But the pear tree was as lovely as ever and as full of flower and as still.

Taking the Veil

It seemed impossible that anyone should be unhappy on such a beautiful morning. Nobody was, decided Edna, except herself. The windows were flung wide in the houses. From within there came the sound of pianos, little hands chased after each other and ran away from each other, practising scales. The trees fluttered in the sunny gardens, all bright with spring flowers. Street boys whistled, a little dog barked; people passed by, walking so lightly, so swiftly, they looked as though they wanted to break into a run. Now she actually saw in the distance a parasol, peach-coloured, the first parasol of the year.

Perhaps even Edna did not look quite as unhappy as she felt. It is not easy to look tragic at eighteen, when you are extremely pretty, with the cheeks and lips and shining eyes of perfect health. Above all, when you are wearing a French blue frock and your new spring hat trimmed with cornflowers. True, she carried under her arm a book bound in horrid black leather. Perhaps the book provided a gloomy note, but only by accident; it was the ordinary Library binding. For Edna had made going to the Library an excuse for getting out of the house to think, to realize what had happened, to decide somehow what was to be done now.

An awful thing had happened. Quite suddenly, at the theatre last night, when she and Jimmy were seated side by side in the dress-circle, without a moment's warning – in fact, she had just finished a chocolate almond and passed the box to him again – she had fallen in love with an actor. But – fallen – in – love . . .

The feeling was unlike anything she had ever imagined before. It wasn't in the least pleasant. It was hardly thrilling. Unless you can call the most dreadful sensation of hopeless misery, despair, agony and wretchedness, thrilling. Combined with the certainty that if that actor met her on the pavement after, while Jimmy was fetching their cab, she would follow him to the ends of the earth, at a nod, at a sign, without giving another thought to Jimmy or her father and mother or her happy home and countless friends again . . .

The play had begun fairly cheerfully. That was at the chocolate-almond stage. Then the hero had gone blind. Terrible moment! Edna had cried so much she had to borrow Jimmy's folded, smooth-feeling handkerchief as well. Not that crying mattered. Whole rows were in tears. Even the men blew their noses with a loud trumpeting noise and tried to peer at the programme instead of looking at the stage. Jimmy, most mercifully dry-eyed – for what would she have done without his handkerchief? – squeezed her free hand, and whispered 'Cheer up, darling girl!' And it was then she had taken a last chocolate almond to please him and passed the box again. Then there had been that ghastly scene with the hero alone on the stage in a deserted room at twilight, with a band playing outside and the sound of cheering coming from the street. He had tried – ah! how painfully, how pitifully! – to grope his way to the window. He had succeeded at last. There he stood holding the curtain while one beam of light, just one beam, shone full on his raised sightless face and the band faded away into the distance . . .

It was – really, it was absolutely – oh, the most – it was simply – in fact, from that moment Edna knew that life could never be the same. She drew her hand away from Jimmy's, leaned back, and shut the chocolate box for ever. This at last was love!

Edna and Jimmy were engaged. She had had her hair up for a year and a half; they had been publicly engaged for a year. But they had known they were going to marry each other ever since they walked in the Botanical Gardens with their nurses, and sat on the grass with a wine biscuit and a piece of barley-sugar each for their tea. It was so much an accepted thing that Edna had worn a wonderfully good imitation of an engagement-ring out of a cracker all the time she was at school. And up till now they had been devoted to each other.

But now it was over. It was so completely over that Edna found it difficult to believe that Jimmy did not realize it too. She smiled wisely, sadly, as she turned into the gardens of the Convent of the Sacred Heart and mounted the path that led through them to Hill Street. How much better to know it now than to wait until after they were married! Now it was possible that Jimmy would get over it. No, it was no use deceiving herself; he would never get over it! His life was wrecked, was ruined; that was inevitable. But he was young . . . Time, people always said, Time might make a little, just a little difference. In forty years when he was an old man, he 81 might be able to think of her calmly – perhaps. But she, – what did the future hold for her?

Edna had reached the top of the path. There under a new-leafed tree, hung with little bunches of white flowers, she sat down on a green bench and looked over the Convent flower-beds. In the one nearest to her there grew tender stocks, with a border of blue, shell-like pansies, with at one corner a clump of creamy freesias, their light spears of green criss-crossed over the flowers. The Convent pigeons were tumbling high in the air, and she could hear the voice of Sister Agnes who was giving a singing lesson. *Ah-me*, sounded the deep tones of the nun, and *Ah-me*, they were echoed . . .

If she did not marry Jimmy, of course she would marry nobody. The man she was in love with, the famous actor – Edna had far too much common sense not to realize that would never be. It was very odd. She didn't even want it to be. Her love was too intense for that. It had to be endured, silently; it had to torment her. It was, she supposed, simply that kind of love.

'But, Edna!' cried Jimmy. 'Can you never change? Can I never hope again?'

Oh, what sorrow to have to say it, but it must be said. 'No, Jimmy, I will never change.'

Edna bowed her head; and a little flower fell on her lap, and the voice of Sister Agnes cried suddenly *Ah-no*, and the echo came, *Ah-no* . . .

At that moment the future was revealed. Edna saw it all. She was astonished; it took her breath away at first. But, after all, what could be more natural? She would go into a convent . . . Her father and mother do everything to dissuade her, in vain. As for Jimmy, his state of mind hardly bears thinking about. Why can't they understand? How can they add to her suffering like this? The world is cruel, terribly cruel! After a last scene when she gives away her jewellery and so on to her best friends – she so calm, they so broken-hearted – into a convent she goes. No, one moment. The very evening of her going is the actor's last evening at Port Willin. He receives by a strange messenger a box. It is full of white flowers. But there is no name, no card. Nothing? Yes, under the roses, wrapped in a white handkerchief, Edna's last photograph with, written underneath,

The world forgetting, by the world forgot.

Edna sat very still under the trees; she clasped the black book in her fingers as though it were her missal. She takes the name of Sister Angela. Snip! Snip! All her lovely hair is cut off. Will she be allowed to send one curl to Jimmy? It is contrived somehow. And in a blue gown with a white head-band Sister Angela goes from the convent to the chapel, from the chapel to the convent with something unearthly in her look, in her sorrowful eyes, and in the gentle smile with which they greet the little children who run to her. A saint! She hears it whispered as she paces the chill, wax-smelling corridors. A saint! And visitors to the chapel are told of the nun whose voice is heard above all the other voices, of her youth, her beauty, of her tragic, tragic love. 'There is a man in this town whose life is ruined . . .'

A big bee, golden furry fellow, crept into a freesia, and the 83 delicate flower leaned over, swung, shook; and when the bee flew away it fluttered still as though it were laughing. Happy, careless flower!

Sister Angela looked at it and said, 'Now it is winter.' One night, lying in her icy cell, she hears a cry. Some stray animal is out there in the garden, a kitten or a lamb or – well, whatever little animal might be there. Up rises the sleepless nun. All in white, shivering but fearless, she goes and brings it in. But next morning, when the bell rings for matins, she is found tossing in high fever . . . in delirium . . . and she never recovers. In three days all is over. The service has been said in the chapel, and she is buried in the corner of the cemetery reserved for the nuns, where there are plain little crosses of wood. Rest in Peace, Sister Angela . . .

Now it is the evening. Two old people leaning on each other come slowly to the grave and kneel down sobbing, 'Our daughter! Our only daughter!' Now there comes another. He is all in black; he comes slowly. But when he is there and lifts his black hat, Edna sees to her horror his hair is snow-white. Jimmy! Too late! The tears are running down his face; he is crying *now*. Too late, too late! The wind shakes the leafless trees in the churchyard. He gives one awful bitter cry.

Edna's black book fell with a thud to the garden path. She jumped up, her heart beating. My darling! No, it's not too late. It's all been a mistake, a terrible dream. Oh, that white hair! How could you have done it? She has not done it. Oh, heavens! Oh, what happiness! She is free, young, and nobody knows her secret. Everything is still possible for her and Jimmy. The house they have planned may still be built, the little solemn boy with his hands behind his back watching them plant the standard roses may still be born. His baby sister . . . But when Edna got as far as his baby sister, she stretched out her arms as though the little love came flying through the air to her, and gazing at the garden, at the white sprays on the trees, at those darling pigeons blue against the blue, and the Convent with its narrow windows, she realizes that now at last for the first time in her life – she had never imagined any feeling like it before – she knew what it was to be in love, but – in – love!

MARTIN AMIS · *God's Dice*
HANS CHRISTIAN ANDERSEN · *The Emperor's New Clothes*
MARCUS AURELIUS · *Meditations*
JAMES BALDWIN · *Sonny's Blues*
AMBROSE BIERCE · *An Occurrence at Owl Creek Bridge*
DIRK BOGARDE · *From Le Pigeonnier*
WILLIAM BOYD · *Killing Lizards*
POPPY Z. BRITE · *His Mouth will Taste of Wormwood*
ITALO CALVINO · *Ten Italian Folktales*
ALBERT CAMUS · *Summer*
TRUMAN CAPOTE · *First and Last*
RAYMOND CHANDLER · *Goldfish*
ANTON CHEKHOV · *The Black Monk*
ROALD DAHL · *Lamb to the Slaughter*
ELIZABETH DAVID · *I'll be with You in the Squeezing of a Lemon*
N. J. DAWOOD (TRANS.) · *The Seven Voyages of Sindbad the Sailor*
ISAK DINESEN · *The Dreaming Child*
SIR ARTHUR CONAN DOYLE · *The Man with the Twisted Lip*
DICK FRANCIS · *Racing Classics*
SIGMUND FREUD · *Five Lectures on Psycho-Analysis*
KAHLIL GIBRAN · *Prophet, Madman, Wanderer*
STEPHEN JAY GOULD · *Adam's Navel*
ALASDAIR GRAY · *Five Letters from an Eastern Empire*
GRAHAM GREENE · *Under the Garden*
JAMES HERRIOT · *Seven Yorkshire Tales*
PATRICIA HIGHSMITH · *Little Tales of Misogyny*
M. R. JAMES AND R. L. STEVENSON · *The Haunted Dolls' House*
RUDYARD KIPLING · *Baa Baa, Black Sheep*
PENELOPE LIVELY · *A Long Night at Abu Simbel*
KATHERINE MANSFIELD · *The Escape*